A DOG FOR LIFE

Also by L. S. Matthews

Fish

A DOG FOR LIFE

L. S. Matthews

DELACORTE PRESS

Published by Delacorte Press
an imprint of Random House Children's Books
a division of Random House, Inc.
New York

Originally published in Great Britain in 2006 by Hodder Children's Books

www.randomhouse.com/kids

Educators and librarians, for a variety of teaching tools,
visit us at www.randomhouse.com/teachers

Library of Congress Cataloging-in-Publication Data

Matthews, L. S. (Laura S.)
A dog for life / L. S. Matthews.
p. cm.
Summary: When John, who has a special ability to communicate with animals, finds that his dog, Mouse, is scheduled to go to the pound, he and Mouse decide to run away and find his uncle, who may be able to help them.
ISBN-13: 978-0-385-73366-3 (trade) — ISBN-13: 978-0-385-90381-3 (glb)
ISBN-10: 0-385-73366-6 (trade) — ISBN-10: 0-385-90381-2 (glb)
[1. Human-animal communication—Fiction. 2. Runaways—Fiction.
3. Friendship—Fiction. 4. Dogs—Fiction. 5. England—Fiction.] I. Title.
PZ7.M43367Do 2006
[Fic]—dc22
2006045664

Printed in the United States of America

10 9 8 7 6 5 4 3 2 1

First American Edition

In memory of Mouse

1987–2002

ONE
Truth and Lies

This is the true story of the journey of John Hawkins (that's me) and our dog, Mouse, from way up north to way down south. You've probably heard a mention of it before, but the people that tell the news, they don't tell it right. I never knew that before, until I heard how they told *our* story. They got all sorts of things wrong, and it made me mad.

My mum said that everyone knows the news people always get it wrong. You hear famous people moaning about it all the time. She said, some of the time they just make mistakes, but mostly it's because they tell the story *they* want to tell, or the story people want to hear.

I thought about that and realized it was true; I was always hearing famous people complaining the news stories about them were wrong, and maybe I just hadn't believed them. And it's true that people like the most crazy story, as long as they can believe it. Like, *"Joe got a new bike for Christmas"* won't exactly race around the school, but *"Joe got a new bike for Christmas, but everyone knows his dad stole it"* will. Even if the more exciting version isn't true. But

1

"Joe got a new bike for Christmas, and aliens delivered it to his door" won't work; the person trying to pass that one on is likely to get either no reaction or some pain.

And I worked out long ago that bit about people *not* believing stuff they don't want to hear. Sometimes they just act like they haven't heard. Sometimes they call you a liar. For them, anything is better than trying to believe something they don't understand.

An example of this is when my brother Tom saw a ghost. Not "saw" exactly, because we were leaving a church after a wedding and he was walking a little way ahead, chatting away to someone he thought was a relative, walking next to him. He said afterward he just vaguely noticed it was a man, in a suit, but when you're walking alongside someone, you don't really look at them. We saw him talking to himself, and we called to him, and he looked back at us, and then all around, and asked where the guy had gone.

Mum didn't like it, I could tell, and said Tom must have been imagining things. Tom and I realized later it must have been a ghost. But people don't like ghosts—why, I don't know. Tom said this guy was perfectly friendly before he vanished; though, when he thought about it, he hadn't actually said anything back to Tom. So we shut up about it after that.

We also dreamed the same dreams some nights. We found we even sometimes got *each other's* dreams by mistake, though we couldn't think why—we're not twins or anything; Tom's two years older. Like one day Tom had been playing ball with his mate and that night I had the dream of doing the same thing, but I could tell it was Tom, not me, and in the dream he was irritated about something that wasn't fair. I found this a bit of a boring dream, and told him off the next day, and said could he keep *his* dreams out of *my* dreams, which were much better than his.

Tom said he'd had one about my ant farm being tipped over; but he wasn't interested in the ant farm, and if I'd keep my dreams, he'd try and keep his.

We never worked out why this happened, and of course, there wasn't really anything we could do about it. But we didn't tell people—including Mum—because we'd tried before, and they seemed to get cross with us, or think we were lying.

The same sort of thing was true about Mouse. Mouse had been a puppy when we were young, and she was called Mouse because she had squeaked like one. Of course, me and Tom, we understood everything she said and she felt the same. We could talk out loud to her or just by thinking the words, and we'd hear her talk right back, in our heads. She was just a person like anyone—maybe a bit cleverer than most—who happened to have paws and fur and so on; she could run faster and play ball better than both of us.

We found out, as we got older, that we could talk with most dogs, though it took a little more time and effort, as other dogs weren't used to doing this with humans. But we slowly realized that other people thought "dog" like they thought "cabbage"; it was another species entirely that you couldn't communicate with or anything. When Mouse did stuff, they said we'd trained her. If the tough kids think you're lying, you're liable for a beating, so we kept quiet, but it was hard, because it seemed unfair on Mouse. The good thing was, Tom pointed out, she really didn't care. She had humans all sized up, and if she could cope with their small brain limitation, so could we.

Now, the reason I'm writing this is because Mum said, what you can do is write the truth yourself. Some of these famous people do that and call it an autobiography, or memoirs. Then you get your say. So that's what I'm doing. And I don't lie, so all this really is true. Well, sometimes you'll see I had to cover myself with a story or two, on my journey, but I'm not hiding that from you, and like I said, sometimes you have to go along with people and tell them what they want to hear.

The truth of the story is, me and Mouse made the journey to save my brother, Tom. But the newspapers wouldn't understand that. You'll maybe have just heard about me "running away with a pet dog" and so on. Me and Mouse and Tom, we knew the truth, but no one seemed to listen. Now it's different. That's why I'm writing this.

We lived with our mum, way up north, like I said, in a rickety old house all by itself, with small windows and low doors, because it was built long, long ago and I suppose it never fell down and no one bothered to build a new one.

Back when the house was born, people found it hard to heat houses and also they were smaller in height (the people, I mean), so that's why the windows were small, to keep the heat in, and you had to watch your head on the ceiling. The walls were thick—again, this was supposed to keep the heat in, but it made the place even smaller on the inside and the place was always cold, just the same.

We weren't too far away from the little village, which was lucky, because though we had a few sheep and chickens and grew fruit and vegetables, Mum needed to work, for our clothes and the heating and so on, and the old car. We didn't use it very much, but she said she liked to have it in case of an emergency, because we were a long way from the nearest hospital, and it worried her, being so far away from everything.

The mountains rose up away behind us; the few houses in the village and scattered around like ours were built on either stony, thin soil, or marshy, peaty soil. We had the stony kind, which Mum said was better for the sheep, to avoid foot rot, but not so good for putting any weight on the lambs or for growing the vegetables.

People came sometimes from far away to look at the mountains, and climb them too. No one local did; everyone knew they were dangerous, and a person could easily slip and fall and be killed. Mum pointed out that the little graveyard was mostly full of visitors; they had the best headstones, I noticed. So me and Tom and Mouse sneaked off secretly when we went climbing and exploring, so as not to worry her. You saw the best birds and all kinds of things up on the mountains and, after all, what else was there to do?

Mum probably worried so much about us slipping off a mountain and the possible-emergency-being-far-from-a-hospital thing because Dad had died in an accident when Mouse was a pup, I was about six, and Tom was eight. Of course, Dad didn't slip off a mountain, nor was he far from a hospital at the time—which did him no good anyway—but that's not how Mum's brain works.

Dad was a clever man, from the south, and both these things seemed to be viewed with a bit of suspicion by locals, Gran (my mum's mum), and even possibly Mum. He had lots of "learning"—degrees I think—in things which were of no use when he came up here to the north with Mum. He had to work in the nearest big town, and then it was just piling up boxes in a factory, and he'd just been moved up to being able to drive the forklift, when someone overstacked the piles of boxes and they fell on him, and he was crushed to death.

Mum always seemed a bit cross with him for this; Gran used to say, "And what good did all that learning do him *then?*" in a satisfied way, which again, doesn't make much sense, but you just had to keep quiet and go with it. Certainly, it left Mum in a bit of a mess, with two young kids and animals and vegetables and all, out in the middle of nowhere; though I don't suppose Dad went and got crushed on purpose, and in any case, we thought she was the one who'd wanted to live there. It's lucky we were fairly close to the village, and maybe people were a bit sorry for her, so that she got the plum job working in the only shop, which kept us going.

It wasn't great, but it was a life, and like lots of things, you only realize you're happy like that when the thing comes along which threatens to tear it all apart forever.

The thing was bigger than the great mountains which towered up behind our house and pierced the clouds in the sky, but it wasn't beautiful, or solid, like them, and no one else could see it unless you told them it was there. Then they saw it too, and their faces went white, and the shock closed up their mouths. It was slimy and dark and you couldn't get ahold of it; there was no way to deal with it. It was the monster of all your nightmares, and it was called the Diagnosis.

TWO
The Diagnosis

It's hard to remember when we really noticed Tom becoming properly ill. He seemed to have a bug, then one after the other, then it became hard to see a gap between them, and him getting better. He was always sick, and became less fun. His dreams were of spiders running all over him and, sharing them, I woke in a sweat, swatting at the bedcovers.

I remember the day he stood up and just went down again, folded at the knees, *flump* on the floor. Mum picked him up almost without saying anything, put him in the car, and I crawled in alongside him. We were all silent as she battled with the ignition and accelerator—the old car was always a bit unhappy about starting—but today it seemed, like us, to know she meant business, and spluttered into life out of fear.

I sat in the waiting room as Tom and Mum swept into the doctor's surgery ahead of everyone else, Joan the receptionist helping to carry Tom in.

I waited for what seemed an age, feeling a bit forgotten

but not minding, because I knew Tom was most important at the moment. Then the doctor stuck his snowy white head out of the door of his room and called Joan. She bustled past again into the room, and was out in a moment, heading for her phone. I heard her call an ambulance and my middle suddenly felt empty and my feet as if they were stuck to the floor.

Suddenly, she looked across at me, and put a smile over the worry on her face.

"Don't worry, John," she said, "it's not as bad as all that. The doctor just wants some tests done that he can't do here, and he thought it would be easier for your mum if the ambulance took Tom to the hospital, instead of your car making the big journey."

"Oh," I said. I wanted to know if me and Mum would go in the ambulance too, but I didn't know if that was allowed. Then Mum came out of the doctor's room and she looked at me as if she had found herself on another planet, and most surprising of all, *I* was there.

Joan looked across at her. "Is there anyone I can call who could take John for you?"

"Um, that's an idea. And the car, I don't know what to do about that. . . ."

"The car will be fine here till you can collect it."

"I want to come," I said firmly. For one thing, Tom would rather I was there. For another, riding in an ambulance would be a first.

"No, no," said Mum, shaking her head. "The state of the hospital, you'll probably end up catching something too. Besides, I expect we'll have to sit and wait for hours to be seen. Very boring for you. There's Gran, I suppose. . . ."

So that's how it ended up. Joan was kind enough to run me to Gran's house, which could be a bit boring, but I didn't mind today. She looked smaller than ever, but she gave me an extra-big bone-breaking hug, and rubbed her soft cheek against mine. Then she got out the crayons and paper I'd played with since I was about two, and we didn't say much while I colored and colored, as carefully as I could, as if it might be the last time I did that, as if maybe Tom's life depended on it, and we waited and waited, with the smell of furniture polish as heavy in the house as the *thunk, thunk* of the big old clock.

Gran bustled around every so often, making cups of tea, washing up, cooking us a big stew as night came pressing at the windows. I drew the curtains against the dark, and cleared the grate of old ashes, and made up a fire. We ate slowly, in old armchairs with worn patches in the brown

11

fabric of the arms, the gold of the firelight making everything seem rich, warm. Gran sighed, "Ah, well," every now and then, and ruffled my hair once or twice as she carried a plate away.

Finally, the sound of the phone smacked the silence out of its way, and you knew by its tone that it was important. Gran got to it in a curious way, as if she wanted to hurry, but was trying not to.

She listened, she asked questions, looking at me as she did so, and speaking clearly so I could hear. "They're keeping him in? How long for? Ah, just overnight . . . What tests? Oh. Do they have an idea? No, they don't like to worry people, I know. Well, that's right, my dear, he's in the best place. John's fine, no trouble, eaten up all his dinner . . ." with a wink at me, as I had a big pile of stew left cold in the bowl on my lap . . . "So he can sleep here, and we'll see you both tomorrow. . . ." She smiled at me to make sure I'd got the last bit.

"He'll be back home tomorrow, they're only keeping him in to do some tests. So that's good."

"Then he'll be better?" I asked.

"The tests are to find what's wrong with him. When they get the results, well, then they'll really know what's the best treatment and medicine, and then he should get better. Might take a while, John. You'll have to be patient."

But, to cut a long story short, when Tom came home, and the doctors looked at the test results, it wasn't quite that simple. Tom was mostly in bed, tired all the time and bored out of his mind. I told him what Gran had said. "They find what's the matter—that's the diagnosis—then they pick the right medicine, then you'll be better. Not long to wait." And Mouse came in with her whiskery eyebrows all quizzical and asked what he was doing in bed all day, and teased him by sneezing in his ear and trying to lick his feet. Then she went a bit serious when we told her, and curled up on the floor looking worried, and said she'd wait there for the diagnosis.

Mum had to go back to the hospital to hear it, risking the car, and when she came back home she'd got Gran with her—she must have picked her up on the way. Mum was all bleary and red around the eyes, and Gran was doing her "in control" thing, but it was scary to see the shake in her hand which gave her away. The diagnosis was that Tom would have to have lots of horrible medicine, and go to the hospital a lot, and it would take a long time before he was better.

We had to get a bit firm with Mum to spit out the whole truth of it. What they really meant was, *if* Tom got better. He might not get better at all. No, they didn't mean he'd stay ill if he didn't get better. He would die.

All of us ended up somehow cross with someone, and crying. All of us, that is, except Tom, who didn't look that surprised, and as usual, just looked very tired. "Tom, you'll be all right," I said to him firmly, sniffing and wiping the back of my hand across my nose. "I'm sorry the medicine will be horrible, but it'll work."

Gran's voice wobbled. "Of course Tom will be all right," she said, patting his hand. "Everyone knows that fighters pull through. Tom is tough and a fighter, aren't you? The main thing is to keep cheerful, keep the spirits up."

"Yes," Tom said, "I've read about it. Scientifically proven. So you'd better all stop crying around me and start cracking a few jokes."

Mum suddenly looked down at Mouse. She had jumped up to say hello to everyone when they came in, listened worriedly to the diagnosis, and now wound herself into a sable curl next to Tom's bed again.

"Oh dear," said Mum, and looked at Gran, "there's another thing. Tom mustn't have any risk of infection around him while he's being treated. They say the dog has to go."

Me and Tom looked at her in horror. Mouse said she knew it, she'd known it all along, and pushed her black leather nose tighter into her white-socked paws.

"Go where?" Tom squeaked.

"We'll find her a good home, I'm sure," said Mum.

"Didn't you say the hospital was full of bugs anyway?" I asked, outraged. "That place must be far more dangerous than poor old Mouse!"

"Don't make it harder than it has to be," said Gran. "The doctor has said absolutely no dog."

Gran, while she is fine in most ways, is unfortunately antidog. We knew we couldn't ask her to take Mouse.

"Can someone look after her, and we'll take her back when I'm better?" asked Tom.

"It might be a year, Tom. I can try, but I don't think people like giving them back, once they've grown fond of them. Anyway, she's getting on. I don't think she wants all that to-ing and fro-ing. Let's not talk about it now. The lady from the dog pound will come and take her on Monday." And Mum and Gran hurried out of the room, unable to deal with Tom's accusing eyes.

"The pound!" said Tom. "Hell, couldn't she do any better than that? She'll only have a few days if no one chooses her."

Mouse faced us squarely and asked what we intended to do about it.

"At least a charity might have hung on to her and found a good home," I said, "but that's not the point. You can't just go around giving Mouse away, like an old table or something. They might as well do that to me!"

"True," said Tom dully, "I bet there's more risk of infection from you than Mouse. But they don't get it and they never will. Now I feel worse than ever. It'll be bad missing Mouse for any time at all, but at least if I knew she was safe and would be back, that would be worth getting better for."

"Taking Mouse away forever might be the thing that tips the balance," I agreed. "Can't we persuade them your getting better depends on it? Isn't there someone else she could stay with?"

"Can't think of anyone. Ask Mum." Tom sniffed sadly, and he turned and faced the wall.

"Come on," I said to Mouse, "you've got good eyes. Do that look at Mum and Gran and back me up."

But it was no go.

"Haven't we a single relative who might take her? Didn't you say Dad had a brother who came to the funeral?" I tried.

"Your uncle David, but he's no good. He lives down south, as far from here as you can get. He hardly speaks, a very taciturn man," said Gran, putting her lips together disapprovingly. "He of all people wouldn't be bothered with a dog. And if he were, he's much too far away."

"Tom is very upset," I tried. "He shouldn't be upset. It'll stop him getting better. If Mouse—"

"Well," interrupted Mum, "if that's the case, you can get him to see how unimportant the dog is, take his mind off it. I told your dad we didn't need a dog, but there was no reasoning with him. Now look at the trouble it's causing."

"She helps with the sheep, when they escape. And she does keep the foxes away," I reminded her.

"If I'd wanted that, I'd get a proper collie, not some mongrel," snapped Mum. Gran put her arm around her shoulders.

"Leave it now, John," she said. "Your mother has Tom to worry about without going on about a dog."

I went back to Tom to tell him what they'd said.

"How ironic," said Tom, coughing slightly. "They don't see they *have* to worry about the dog, if they worry about me."

Mouse had followed me into Tom's room. *I tried the eyes thing, but it didn't work on them,* she explained to Tom. *Obviously you'll have a plan?*

She could be quite bossy like that.

THREE
The Plan

"We have to take her away from here," said Tom.

"*I* have to, you mean," I said.

Both of you stop staring at me and talking about me as if I wasn't here, said Mouse, crossly. *And anyway, I don't want to go.*

"What you want," said Tom firmly, "is to stay here, and not to be got rid of—I know. That is not a choice which is available. We all want everything to stay the same, Mouse. No one wants me to be ill either, but it can't be helped. So we have to do the next best thing. You can't stay here, but you won't be got rid of. John will take you somewhere safe. . . ."

. . . and stay with me?

". . . and stay with you as long as he has to."

Mouse didn't look entirely happy about this, probably because she was in on all the thought conversation, which included me wondering where I was supposed to be taking her and how I would manage to stay there.

It came to me in a flash, and instantly I knew Tom was thinking the same thing, because that was the only place, the only person . . .

"Uncle David?" I asked.

Tom nodded slowly. He was starting to look tired. "Can't think of anyone else. But it's miles and miles. I wish I could do it. . . ."

"I can do it. Miles and miles is good. Not much Mum and Gran can do about it once I've got Mouse there."

Mouse wagged her tail slowly and looked from Tom to me and back again. *Uncle David, that's the brother, isn't it, the brother of Dad?*

"Yes," I said carefully, "but we have no idea what he'll think. . . ."

Dad was a good leader, said Mouse. *I remember, though I was only a pup. He found me and brought me here. The brother is worth a try.*

"Should I find Mum's address book and phone him?" I said to Tom, sitting on the edge of the bed. His eyes glittered out at me from their dark circles. His lips seemed paler.

"No. If you warn him, the grown-ups'll stop it. You speak to him, and he will *have* to speak to Mum. It's like a code of honor with adults. If you don't warn him, there's nothing he can do about it and it's not his fault. But you do need the address book. And a map, and train times, and everything you can think of. Sneak it all somehow, and come back after dinner for a planning session."

"Will do," I said, and headed for the door. He needed to sleep. I turned to see if Mouse was coming.

Tom reached out one hand and weakly stroked the top of her head. "Mouse, you could give him a hand. No one would ever suspect you of stealing."

I should hope not, said Mouse. *But you're right, I'd be a great thief—all for a good cause, of course.*

I had only managed to find a bit of paper and a pen to make a list with, before Mum called me for dinner.

We ate in the kitchen; today it was warm and steamy with the scent of homemade bread making your mouth water. Mum had laid out a big plate of it in slices as thick as your arm, and there was a brick of soft yellow butter from the neighbors' farm, a present from kind people which said, "We have heard your news and we are sorry," without anyone having to speak. Mum had filled the old blue china dish with hot, brown, hard-boiled eggs, and next to that was a big glass dish bundled with green salad leaves, glistening from their rinsing, and red tomatoes flashing out among them, sweet and still warm from the glass lean-to where Mum tended them.

This was what Mum called a lazy meal, meaning, easy for her to serve because you put it all together on your plate yourself, but we loved them best. It slowed me down for a second, though, to think of Tom in bed without the hunger within him to enjoy this.

But I had to get on with collecting things to make our plan ready for when he woke up, so I ate quickly, and scraped my plate all tidy. Then Mum was out the door to take the washing in, and I took my chance.

I found the address book, an old and tiny thing in creased black leather, crumpled like a little bat in the dark corner where we kept the telephone. Mum had few friends and relatives, so she'd probably had this book forever.

I decided to jot the name and address onto my bit of paper, rather than take the book, which might be missed. I was quick but I copied carefully, because the words were strange to me.

"Did you find the map, Mouse?" I asked.

Yes, she said, *but it's a bit big. I could get it out and bring it, but I'm likely to make a bit of a noise. Come here, I'll show you,* and she led me to the bookshelf at the back of the damp sitting room and nudged a big book of road maps with her nose.

I tucked it under my arm. Then I took the lot up to Tom's room before Mum got back in with the washing. He was just waking up and I managed to stow the bits under his bed as Mum came up the stairs.

"John? You shouldn't really wake Tom up. . . ."

She peered in the doorway and we grinned at her.

"Well—I suppose I do want him to eat something. How are you feeling? Can I bring you a bite now?"

Her face looked so quivery and anxious, I knew Tom was just pleasing her when he said, "Yes, thanks, the bread smells lovely."

She turned to go, then swung round again, her eyes on us, stern as an old ewe guarding its lamb.

"I see that dog's in here. Come on, what did I tell you both? Mouse, out!"

Mouse walked out, all humble. Another thing she did well.

Silently, we told her we'd leave the door open.

We heard Mum clinking plates onto a tray down-stairs, but before she appeared again there was the swift clickety-clack of claws on the wooden stairs and Mouse shot into the room again. I pulled up the bedcover from where it met the floor and she dived underneath, as Mum's slow tread came up toward us from the kitchen.

Once she'd gone, and Tom was propped on his pillows with the tray of food in front of him, Mouse twitched her nose out from under the bed and sneezed.

I reached for the map and paper and pen and dumped them on the bed.

"That's all I've got at the moment. I was going to look for a train timetable, like you said, but I don't reckon we've got one, do you?"

"No," said Tom. "The closest they go from would be—Highwick?"

"S'pose so. I reckon I could walk there. . . ."

"You'd have to be careful no one saw you."

"Go across the fields. What about the money for the ticket?"

"We'll have to raid the money boxes. I've got some from my birthday. What about you?"

"Pocket money. How much will it cost, do you reckon?"

Tom knew about as much as I did, which meant not one thing, but as the older brother, he had to be better at making a guess.

He looked up at the ceiling, narrowed his eyes, and pulled a crumb of bread off the hunk on his plate. I waited.

"No idea," he sighed finally, "but I bet it will be more than we have."

"I can ask when I get there, then go as far as I can on the money and walk the rest."

"Hmm," he said. "Well, let's look at the map. Give us that address."

I passed it all over to him, and then we had to unstick the bread from the back cover of the road map, and scrape the butter off with our fingers.

Tom was quiet for a bit as he turned the pages, and Mouse came out offering to help clear up any food accidents without even being asked.

"Well?" I asked at last.

"I've found the place—but we'll have to look on the map of the whole country to see where we are and how to get there. Here." He flicked a piece of eggshell from the page. I twisted sideways on the edge of the bed to see.

"This is better—there's us," *tap tap* at the top of the map, "and right down here, near the sea at the bottom— that's Uncle David."

"Like you said—about as far from each other as we could be. It looks OK on a map . . . ," I said slowly.

"Because the map is very, very small," Tom said in a big brother voice, and patted my head. I wriggled away.

"That's not fair. You know I can't hit you if you're ill. I'm warning you, I'm going to save up all the punches till you're better."

"Yeah, yeah," yawned Tom. "It will take hours on a train, but you're going to have to do it like that. You musn't wander around the country or try and get lifts. There are all kinds of weird people about."

I will protect John, said Mouse, standing up from under the bed and wagging her tail. We'd forgotten she was there.

"That's a point. I hope they take dogs on the train," I said.

"I'm sure they do," said Tom, then added to Mouse, "And as for protecting John, well, out in the dark, mad killers go about with axes and knives and guns."

Oh, well, we must take our chances then, said Mouse. *But I'll do my best to scare off people who try to hurt John, so long as they are frightened of dogs, and I don't really have to bite—only as a last resort—and they aren't too big, and don't have axes or knives and so on.* She lay down again and put her nose on her paws and then, looking thoughtful, added: *Do people like that only want to kill other people, or do they sometimes want to kill animals, say, dogs?* She looked worriedly at us and pulled her tail more tightly round herself.

"Tom is being horrible, Mouse, and if he scares me too much, I won't go, and then what will happen? Just ignore him."

"Seriously, though, John," said Tom, "we do need to know that information. About the train and so on. Suppose they don't take dogs or it's too much money?"

"What if I go, as if I'm doing the real thing, setting off on the journey—and if everything is fine, me and Mouse carry on—otherwise, we come back and no one will be any the wiser?" I said.

"A recon mission and Operation Save Dog all in one," said Tom thoughtfully. "Good idea. You can say you're going over to Michael's or something and staying for lunch—then if you do carry on with the plan, no one will miss you for ages. But don't go if you are going to end up stranded in the middle of nowhere. You musn't be in danger, either of you." He looked sternly at me.

"And what we do if it's no go and I have to come back, I don't know," I said.

Tom shrugged. "Face that if it comes to it. Let's make a list of what you need to take."

Number one: Dog, said Mouse. *Number two: Food for dog. I'm not fussy, you don't have to take something special for me—I'll eat human food. Number three: Big bowls of water for dog* . . .

I gave her a shove.

"She has a point, though," said Tom. "Water's a terrible thing to carry. Heavy. I'd take an empty bottle and use a lunch box for the bowl, and hope you find a tap somewhere. If you manage to get a train most or all of the way, it's only going to be a day's traveling, surely."

"Where's the nearest station to Uncle David's at the other end?" I asked.

Tom checked the map.

"There's Dunchester or . . . what's that say? Axmouth? Both look about the same distance away."

"Doesn't look far to walk from there," I said, peering over his shoulder. Tom measured on the map with his fingers, then, trying to keep them at the same distance apart, put them near our own village.

"You must get used to maps, John," he said. "It *looks* like you have to walk five centimeters. It's *really* the same distance as from here to, say, Stowton, which is still twenty or so miles. Maybe you can phone him and ask for a lift when you get to the station."

"Maybe," I said, thinking of an angry guy at the other end of the phone, then the police turning up.

Mouse looked at me.

He is Dad's brother. He won't be angry. He will like us. He knows the family. He is of the family.

"I hope you're right," I said to her.

Tom tapped my paper.

"List. Clean socks. Food and drink. Money. Uncle David's address and phone number. Our address and phone number. Wear lots of warm clothes and your hat. Don't carry anything else, it would be too heavy. If you get too warm, you take stuff off and you've room in the bag for it."

I hope I'm not in this train for a long day without a walk, said Mouse.

"You will have to change trains, I think," said Tom. "There will be a chance then to stretch your legs. If you ask someone, there might be buses which are cheaper." He was suddenly keen. "You must take this page with the map of the whole country. Then you can see the towns which are on your route. I know it's wrong to tear books but . . ." and he carefully tore out the page and passed it to me. Then he sat back and looked tired again. I stood up and moved the tray of tousled food so that he could lie down.

"Oh, I wish it was me going," he murmured. "Or best of all, both of us together. Wouldn't that be something?"

"You know, it would be great," I started to say, but Mouse put in, *You'd only argue. Is that it? I want my dinner now, and when are we going? Tomorrow?*

I looked at Tom. His eyelids were lowering. Out of the window, the sun was sinking, the flowers were closing up their faces for evening.

"Yes, Mouse. Tomorrow."

FOUR
The Problem with Plans and Life

I was careful to get up at a normal sort of time for summer break. It was that tail end of summer when the light, the tips of your fingers, and the scents in the air somehow tell you it's turning into autumn. I packed up my bag and told Mum I was going looking for berries with Michael. After about an hour, which seemed like a year, as I went through the act of picking berries (on my own) behind one of the thickets, I trudged back with red, black, and blue smudges on my fingers and the corners of my mouth, and scratches on the backs of my hands. I put the berries down in the kitchen, and asked Mum if it was OK to go over to Michael's for the rest of the day and have lunch there.

Mum was a bit flitty, up and down the stairs to Tom, cleaning things that didn't look like they needed it, so she seemed happy enough for me to go, and even forgot to notice I didn't say when I'd be back.

Me and Mouse said goodbye to Tom, and he made sure I had the money and so on, and made me promise not to get lost; to give up and come back if I was in any danger; and to try and phone.

Then Mouse surprised both of us by saying, *And of course, you won't need the phone to talk to me.* Tom asked her why not, and she said, *Well, we'll just talk to each other like this. How far away I am won't make any difference.* Tom and I looked at each other.

"Does that *work*?" I asked.

Mouse looked surprised. *Of course it works. You didn't know? I thought you just never particularly needed to talk to me when you were at school.*

"Well, I don't suppose we did," said Tom. "That's handy. We will try and keep in touch like that then. Be careful now, both of you," and his voice caught a bit.

"I'll probably find the fare is hundreds of pounds and be back later in any case," I said, and we didn't know what to say next, so we shook hands and then laughed at ourselves, and then I was downstairs and out the front door, Mouse rushing ahead as always. As I walked along the path, the nerves made my heart feel high up and light in my chest, and my feet feel weightless on the ground, so I seemed to bounce along like an astronaut. And as I stepped over the stile, I thought that if I didn't hang on to the wooden post, I would soar and fly away across the fields. I wondered if I looked odd, unnatural. No one called, no one shouted "Stop!"

I didn't look back.

Once beyond the thicket, the valley stretched out below us for miles, green and gold, with tiny homesteads dotted here and there, and blue smoke from a distant fire smudging a line before the next great hill. On its flank the houses clustered, and you could see roads flashing between them, and there, running away between distant bridges and tunnels, you could just catch a glimpse of train tracks.

I pointed.

"The railway, Mouse. The train runs along it. Highwick. We have to get there. Doesn't look too far, does it?"

No, easy. We just go steady, she said, and trotted on impatiently, her tail low and serious.

It was one of those walks where you feel at first as if you could go on forever—maybe because we were heading downhill, now I think about it. I found myself figuring out what was the halfway point—and to be honest, when you start doing that, you should realize that the walk must be wearing on you. When we got to that—a hedge alongside one of the bigger farms—I pulled off my hat and rolled up my coat and managed to stuff them in my bag, while Mouse, panting, looked impatient. I looked at the little town, which was now above us. It did look closer, but I wasn't sure it was halfway closer. Somewhere behind the hedge a cow mooed and coughed.

Mouse pushed on ahead of me, and I knew she was being kind to me when she kept stopping to sniff things, allowing me to catch up.

I was looking at where my feet were going, as it was quite a steep climb in parts, so it was a nice surprise when I looked up and saw the sides of houses, the fences of back gardens. Mouse had seen a proper pavement footpath with a metal rail and was sensibly heading for it.

I slipped underneath it and joined her on the path. No one seemed to be around. *This way?* Mouse asked.

"We need to find the station," I said. "The place where the train stops so we can get on it. If we get into the middle of town, there should be a sign."

I hoped. I didn't know. I didn't want to ask anyone if I could avoid it. I wasn't sure how often kids and dogs got trains, especially on their own.

Does the station smell a bit like where they mend the car? said Mouse. *Because there's something like that this way. We may find it before we get to the middle of town. Of course, it could just be a place where they mend cars.*

"I should think it would smell a bit like that. I haven't

33

been before. We'll keep our eyes open," I said, hoping we'd be lucky, because I had found that walk a bit longer than I'd expected.

I followed Mouse up the path, and it became a little road with small, neat houses on either side. Then the road ended by meeting a bigger road. Cars were whizzing along in both directions. A few people were walking the sidewalks in a purposeful way. I felt their curious glances. Mouse was determinedly taking the turn to the right, sniffing the air rather than the ground. She was hurrying, getting further ahead of me.

"Hold up, Mouse," I said, realizing something. She waited.

What? I'm fairly sure this is the way. Unless you've seen a sign . . .

"No, it's not that. It's you. I haven't got a leash, people think it's odd. They probably think I'm nuts and you're going to run in front of a car. You'll have to walk at my heel. Sorry."

Oh, all right. I hate that. I have to do a funny kind of walk to go that slow. Try and walk fast, would you, and don't tread on my paws.

She slunk to my side. Now the only looks we got were

slightly impressed ones from people who noticed there was no leash when they got close enough to see.

"Look on the bright side, Mouse—they think you are really clever and obedient, doing this," I said, to cheer her up.

Clever and obedient! she snorted, and rammed hard against my leg at a crossing, so I nearly fell over her. *You love it because they think* you *are the clever one, training a dog so well! As for obedient . . . This way! I can't believe you can't smell it.*

"Well, I believe I can, now you mention it. A bit. And anyway, yes, there's the sign. Highwick Station!"

Now that we were crossing the road and heading beneath the sign into the station, my stomach went all churny. All the things we didn't know, that was the problem. What if they didn't let dogs on? What if it cost hundreds of pounds? But heading back home honestly seemed worse than going on with the journey, scary though that was.

Once through the big iron archway, there was a parking lot, a wooden fence you couldn't see over, and a big old brick building with a sign saying TICKET OFFICE above the door. Remembering Mouse and Tom relying on me, I pulled up my chest, sucked in my breath, crossed to the door, and walked in.

No one was there, it seemed—but through the big windows, I saw people standing on a platform. I went up to the little glass window marked TICKET SALES/INQUIRIES, still seeing no one behind the counter. Suddenly, an oldish man with gray hair turning white and a dark blue uniform appeared, as if he had some kind of sensor for customers.

He didn't even say, "Yes?" or "How can I help you?"— just looked at me expectantly over the top of his glasses.

I felt suddenly small and sweaty. There were ears of grass seed sticking to my trousers, I noticed now, and I wondered if I had got rid of all the berry juice on my face.

"I need a ticket for the train," I said, pulling myself together and trying to speak up, though my voice came out in a loud squeak.

"Where to?"

I had forgotten there were probably lots of trains, going to lots of different places.

"Um." I rustled the paper out of my pocket. This wasn't going well. People seemed to be expected to know these things straight away.

"Dunchester, or, er, Axmouth?"

He looked at me—puzzled, but kind.

"Are you sure? Which one? Can't say I've heard of either of them. Let's have a look at your bit of paper."

I passed it under the glass window to him. It went into a little silver metal bowl which spun suddenly by itself and took the paper to him. I stared at it, then realized he was talking while I must have been gawping like an idiot.

"OK, let's key them in here and see what we get." *Tap, tap, tap* on some gray machine with its back to me. Mouse wandered from my side and started to sniff around the room.

"Right down there! Well, that's a big journey, and a few changes to make. You're traveling on your own?" He peered at me shrewdly through the glass.

"Yes, well, with the dog. That's the other thing. Is she allowed? And does she cost much?" I gave up trying to sound bigger than I was. He was trying to help because he knew I didn't have the faintest idea what I was doing. I would put myself at his mercy.

"The dog's allowed, so long as she doesn't take up space needed for passengers. Just a nominal charge. If the train gets full, you stand with her in the space by the doors, all right? Now, Dunchester or Axmouth, the changes are about the same, the cost is the same. . . ." He looked back to his gray machine.

"Changes?" I asked.

"It means, you have to get off the train, and get on another one to get where you want to go. On the best route, you do that twice." He looked at me sharply. "Someone is meeting you at the other end? Aren't they expecting you at a particular station?"

"They—it's my uncle—they said to phone when I got there. Makes no difference which one," I burbled, tripping over my words.

"Righto, shall I do a ticket for Dunchester then?" he said, looking happier at the sound of an uncle.

"How much would that be?" I asked quickly. He looked surprised, as if I should know that.

"Single or return?"

"What?"

"One way or coming back too?" He adopted the careful tone used by nursery teachers.

"Oh, er, single, please."

"Let's see," more tap tapping, then, sucking in air through his teeth, "sixty-three pounds eighty."

My face fell. I had exactly forty-five pounds and thirty-five pence.

Noticing my expression, he said, "I'd have thought your uncle would have checked the price first and sent the

right money. Or even the ticket itself. Or your mum . . . ,"
he started, pushing his glasses up on his nose and peering
at me intently.

"Maybe I got the town wrong," I said quickly. "Sorry.
Mum thought she'd given me enough. She wanted to see
me onto the train, but she's at the hospital with my
brother. He's sick. Hold on a minute."

You have to be careful with adults. But if you play it
right, you can usually convince them you're just a silly kid
making mistakes.

I thumped the bag off my back and pulled out the map
Tom had torn out of the book. I couldn't say to the man,
how far can I get for this much money? He'd know something wasn't right. I traced the route we'd marked in pen
down the map to the biggest place I could see before Dunchester or Axmouth. It was still a way above them, and of
course, they were a way from Uncle David's actual house,
but it was all I could think of.

"Oh, er, Brigstow? Yes, *that's* what I need the ticket for,"
I said, doing a good impression of remembering, smiling
with embarrassment. "He *lives* somewhere between Dunchester and Axmouth. But he said he'd pick me up from
Brigstow."

"Ah," said the ticket man. "Well, that's good of him. A

fair way for him to drive, but much better for you. You just take the next train to Caerfort, then get a train from there which goes with no changes straight to Brigstow, that's probably why he suggested it. Now, with one change, you shouldn't go wrong. When you get to Caerfort, get off and you'll probably hear the announcement for the Brigstow train, but if not, ask someone. Don't be shy. It'll be ten minutes before it goes, that gives you plenty of time to get to the right platform. Probably platform two. OK?"

I nodded, clutching my map, feeling about five years old. He glanced back at his machine.

"Let's see . . . single to Brigstow, that's thirty-seven pounds fifty, including the dog."

"Thank you, thank you very much," I said, counting out the money.

"There you go, that's more like it," he said, pushing the ticket and my change back to me. "And some left for a snack on the train. Next one is in five minutes, so your mum dropped you in good time. You just go through these doors, and wait on the platform."

People were starting to line up for tickets, so I did what he said. Mouse remembered to stay close to my side and look well-behaved.

"There's a bowl of water for dogs," I pointed out to

40

Mouse. "That's kind of them. It might be your last chance for a drink for a while. I don't know if there's water on the train."

Mouse wandered reluctantly over to the bowl in the shade of the ticket-office wall, sniffed disdainfully, and returned.

Full of other dogs' slobber, she said. *I'm not thirsty in any case.*

Then there was a crackling voice, booming off the walls, announcing the next train. Mouse winced, her half-up and half-down ears twitching.

"This is ours, Mouse. Takes us to Caerfort, then another to Brigstow."

We shuffled forward to join the few passengers waiting nearer the platform's edge. A cheerful distant horn sounded on two notes from along the track, and then the face of the train appeared. As it drew in, with much hissing and grinding, Mouse backed away slightly and her fur raised up for a moment, but she put a brave face on as the doors opened.

Ugh! she said. *The sound of two hundred snakes. Why people put up with these things . . .* But she pressed to my leg as I climbed on and did her best to avoid being trodden on by the other passengers.

The carriage we had boarded was not even a quarter full, so I took a seat by the window and Mouse stood looking worried on the floor next to me. At a whistle blow, the train lurched away. Mouse staggered slightly, then put her front paws on my legs to look out of the window.

Nothing eventful happened, but, never having been on a train, I was quite excited enough. After a while, Mouse, who was fascinated by the ever-changing view of hedgerow, back gardens, and fields, said, *This is good!* A little later, she said her back legs were tired and she took her front half off my lap and circled and lay down on the dusty floor.

I listened carefully to the announcements, because I was scared of missing our stop, but they were garbled and fuzzy. I furiously checked the signs of every station we pulled into, my stomach churning. I felt out of my depth already with this plan. When a ticket inspector came along, I asked him how many stops it was to Caerfort.

"Only two more." He smiled cheerfully, and as if he guessed my fear, "Don't worry, the train terminates there, so you won't be able to miss it. Nice dog you got there." And he moved off down the carriage.

What the heck does he mean, "the train terminates"? said Mouse, stirring slightly. *Does it blow up or something?*

"I think he just means it stops, Mouse. It won't carry us on to somewhere we don't want to go."

But where were we going? Brigstow, in the end. How to get from there to Uncle David's? And I began to worry. I hoped I'd made the right decision. You see, the trouble with all plans is they are like life; you go on what you know, you guess at what's likely to happen, you try your best to be ready for anything, and then something always comes up to throw it all in the air.

What we'd said was, if it was too expensive, I'd give up and go back. Well, the *whole* journey *was* too expensive, but I could at least get a fair part of the way on the money we'd brought. But should I have gone back to Tom?

Fence posts flitting past, the *chickety chunk* of wheels on track.

The trouble was, there was no real Plan B. I suppose that was why I'd carried on. We never worked out a Plan B, and I didn't reckon we'd have come up with one, not before Monday and the dog pound lady's visit. Going back would just mean admitting defeat. I might as well have been signing Mouse's death warrant.

Some things life throws at you, there isn't even time for a Plan A, let alone a Plan B, said Mouse suddenly, lifting her head slightly, and yawning. She'd been listening in on my thoughts. *Like Dad's death. What could we do? If I had been there, well, maybe I could have warned him. Every day I told him I ought to go with him. Don't ask me why they never let me. But at least with Tom there's a chance, there's time for a Plan A. Don't be too hard on yourself about this Plan B thing.*

And she rubbed the side of her face on my hand where it rested on my knee.

She listened for a moment, sniffing toward the window. *A big town. Caerfort is coming up, get ready now. You're not on your own, remember. Get us to Brigstow, I'll help out after that. You'll see. It'll be all right.*

I rubbed her head and got to my feet. Sometimes I forgot that Mouse was older than me, though she didn't carry as many years.

FIVE
Mouse Rescues Bonzo

I won't bore you with the story of the rest of the train part of the journey. It bored me enough by the end of it, I can tell you. We got on the Brigstow train easy enough, though again, my heart was really thumping when I took my place in the next carriage. I was looking for it all to go wrong at any stage. This train got more and more crowded, picking up people at every stop and letting fewer and fewer off. By the time we reached Brigstow, which took hours, me and Mouse were in the little gap by the doors.

We stepped off the train into early evening. This was the part which had worried me the most, but now I was too stiff and tired to care much about anything but moving, getting away from the crowds at the station, finding Mouse something to drink.

At first I thought we'd be more likely to be noticed with so many people about, but it seemed to have the opposite effect. No one looked twice at the boy and the dog passing between them. They were all hurrying too much.

Out of the station and all around us were big roads,

more houses and shops than I had ever seen. The air seemed to be made of what came out of the backs of the cars and buses. So much traffic! I stood for a moment, wondering which way to go.

Grass and water, this way, said Mouse firmly. She was panting with thirst, but kept snapping her mouth shut in disgust at the fumes.

I spun left at the pressure of her body on my calf, and we strode out of the station as fast as we could, until the stiffness in my legs eased up and I got quite a swing going, Mouse jog-trotting slightly ahead.

Along the pavement, past fewer and fewer shops, slightly tattier houses, then left again and we were into a big green area, with a football pitch marked out, goal-posts, and a tired-looking set of swings.

Mouse trotted on, getting further and further ahead of me. *Water*, she said. *River, by the smell of it.*

"You go on, I'll catch up," I said, knowing how thirsty she was. I could see the little bridge away across the field. I could also see kids there, one about my size, and two smaller. I hesitated.

Kids are good, said Mouse. *Get playing. They won't be dangerous. They'll take you to their house and give you dinner, won't they?*

46

"Well," I said. "Ones you're friends with, at home, maybe . . ."

Then make these be your friends, too, she said, breaking into a run and disappearing over the hump of the river-bank.

Typical, I thought. It's not that easy, and it's not like she doesn't know that. Mouse gets on with most dogs, but she's certainly not friends with *all* the ones we meet. Take Mrs. Jones's little fur ball of fury. A big sidestep around their gateway every time, just in case it's open. Even if the gate is shut and you're prepared for it, it makes you jump about a meter in the air; a thousand snarling barks a second at a pitch which slices through your ears, then *clang* as the body hits the metal.

But it turned out I didn't have to try very hard. As I reached the top of the embankment and looked down at the river, which ran encased by man-made, reinforced sides, I was aware first of the smallest child, a girl of only about three years old, making as if to step off the edge into the dark, flowing water.

"No, don't!" I shouted, and flung myself after her.

Too late, she was in the water and underneath the surface in a flash, but I jumped in only a fraction of a second behind her and she'd no sooner disappeared than my hand had the pink hood of her coat and I'd yanked her straight back up again and into my arms.

The water streamed off her face, she gave a little gasp of shock, opened her eyes—which had been screwed shut— and started to cry. I was so relieved she was breathing— though she'd really only had a quick dunking—I just stood there for a moment, keeping my feet steady on the riverbed, my legs freezing in the current.

Only then was I aware of the other children. The older boy—I could see now he was about my age, maybe a bit younger—came rushing along the bank toward us, a long stick in his hand, his kid brother behind him.

"Shiff! Oh no! I told you to stay there!" and as he helped take her from me—I couldn't believe how heavy a three-year-old could seem when you tried to lift them above you onto a bank—"Is she all right? Are you all right, Shiff? Oh, Mum will be mad! Look at your clothes!"

His younger brother—I guessed this pretty easy, as they had almost the same face—stood trying to look interested in the near-drowning of the baby sister, while I got out, dripping and puffing. The oddly named Shiff was now struggling and shivering on the bank, apparently very up- set about something and pointing to the water.

"What's the matter with her? Why did she just step off the bank like that?" I asked the older brother, who was trying to calm her down and sort of wiping at her soaking clothes as if that would magically dry them.

"Bonzo, her fluffy toy dog thing—it's her favorite—she dropped it off the bridge. To see if it could swim. I told her to stand still and I'd try and pull him out with the stick. Do stop crying, Shiff. . . ."

Mouse trotted into view with perfect timing.

It's caught down here, she said, *on some bits of tree. I'll have it out in a jiffy.*

The noise from the wet child was terrible. I pulled my coat out of my bag, stuck it round her shoulders, and looked into her eyes.

"Come and see my doggy rescue Bonzo. Come on."

It worked. The crying stopped instantly, and with her big brother holding her hand firmly and her younger brother trailing behind, we walked along the embankment, following Mouse. Shiff was delighted even before Bonzo was rescued, at the sight of Mouse leaping from the bank into the water.

Mouse swam strongly to where a tree branch had fallen and formed a kind of dam, into which the current had swept all sorts of bits of wood and plastic rubbish; captured before it, in a little eddy, spinning round and round, was poor Bonzo, a brownish, flop-eared lump on his side.

Mouse seized him in her jaws, swam around the dam, and allowed herself to be swept along with the current further downstream.

"She'll get out where the bank slopes down more natural," I explained, in case they worried. Mouse was an expert swimmer.

We walked a little further along, and saw a flash of her foxy color as she made land, and before we could take a step more, she was in front of us, with Bonzo in her jaws.

The little girl stretched out her arms from my big coat, which was wrapped awkwardly around her, all her soaking and tears forgotten in an instant.

"Bonzo!"

I took the toy from Mouse's mouth and squeezed a fair bit of the river from it.

"Thank you, Mouse," I said, and passed it to Shiff.

"Thank you, Mouse!" she repeated delightedly, hugging Bonzo and landing Mouse a rather thumping pat on the head.

There you go, Mouse muttered to me. *Now don't mess it up. Get us an invite to dinner, at least.* And she shook herself right next to me on purpose, and Shiff and her brothers screamed with delight.

There, they just love it. Never fails, she said, before I could tell her off.

"I've got to get dry clothes on anyway," I said to her out loud, without thinking. It was a good mistake to make.

"Come back with us, of course," said the older boy. "And thank you. I don't want to think what would have happened if you hadn't been there. Mum's gonna be mad in any case, but if Shiff had drowned"—he showed the whites of his eyes—"I'd really have been in for it."

How upset *he'd* be, personally, if his kid sister had drowned, I couldn't begin to guess, but I said, "Don't you just hate it when they get so wound up over one little kid?" as a joke, and the little brother, who must have been about five, said, "Yeah, and I mean, she'd still have the two of us left, anyway."

This brought the older boy up a bit short, and he must have realized how they sounded, so he said, "Ocean, that's not very nice. Poor Shiff." Then he turned to me, as I was still reeling from what seemed to be his brother's name. "You must be freezing. D'you want to come back to ours and get dry? Mum will be ever so pleased you saved Shiff." He had deep, serious green eyes which he fixed me with.

"Thanks, er . . . ?"

"Sage."

I managed to fight a giggle.

"Thanks, Sage, I would like that. Where do you live?"

"Only there." He pointed to the fence ahead of us. "We back onto the park. You new here?"

"Just visiting my gran for the day. I was a bit bored. . . ."

I was shocked how easy the lie came. It was lucky it did, because I hadn't thought to have a story ready.

Sage nodded understandingly and pushed open a gate in the fence. We straggled up a garden path, Shiff shuffling with difficulty, my coat dragging on the ground, empty sleeves flapping, Bonzo gripped tight to her chest beneath it. She left little wet footprints and splashes. The garden was a bit overgrown and untidy, but it was nothing compared to the house.

I found myself in what seemed to be a kitchen—judging by the stove and so on—but why they needed big old tins of paint, coils of wire heaped up and escaping all over the place like snakes, and about thirty thousand egg cartons on every available surface in a kitchen, I couldn't guess.

Sage was calling, "Mum? Mum!" and heading along

a hall, but he was being drowned out by Shiff suddenly starting a bout of rather put-on crying and running after him, and Ocean cheerfully calling that Sage had almost killed Shiff. I stood dripping, as I didn't think it polite to follow until asked, and Mouse sniffed doubtfully outside the back door.

Crikey, she said, *this is one weird house. Boiled plants and . . .* sniff sniff *. . . quite complicated poisonous chemicals. I'll stay out here till we know what they are like about dogs.*

I glanced about. Dead things in pots moldered on the windowsill. There *was* a funny smell, now she mentioned it.

"Do you think this is—well, safe?" I asked her.

Hmm. Put it this way, I'd check out the food before you eat it, she said vaguely, wandering away, following some scent in the garden.

At that moment, I heard a woman's shriek.

"Chiffon! Sweetie! Oh my *goodness,* what *happened* to you?"

I made out a wild-haired figure in the hall, snatching the little girl up into her arms. Chiffon, Shiff for short. Of course. Delighted at her mother's reaction, Shiff obliged with some louder wails, but eventually, it seemed, Sage managed to get his explanation out.

"A *boy*? Well, is he *all right*? He's here? *Goodness*, bring him in. . . ." And she rushed into the kitchen, still clutching her daughter, who had stopped crying and looked a bit put out that someone else might be getting attention.

The mum wore her hair long and spidery, with a lot of gray in it, like a web; and although the house looked big and everything, maybe they didn't have much money, because her brightly colored clothes seemed to be made out of old bits of curtain, and other parts were crazily knitted, apparently out of leftover wool. I thought maybe they didn't have much money for heating and so on, because she had layers of clothes all higgledy-piggledy.

"Hello," I said, trying to be polite. "I'm sorry I'm getting your floor wet. Should I stand outside?"

"Don't mind that, it hardly matters in here, does it?" she said, sweeping her hand around to include the chaos, and knocking two egg cartons and a coil of wire from the top of the fridge as she did so.

After we'd unpicked my coat and Shiff's hair from the wire, and battled it and the egg cartons back onto the fridge, all being ever so polite ("Excuse me, if you could just lift your foot a little?" "Oops, sorry, nearly had your eye out there!"), I was sent with Sage up to his room to find a towel and borrow some trousers, while his mum bribed Shiff into the bathroom with the promise that Bonzo could just this once have a bath with her.

Sage's room wasn't too bad, if a bit messy, and they didn't seem so poor after all, because he had a real guitar and drums which came all the way from Africa, and a thing called a rainstick which was just wooden but made a sound like rain when you tipped it, and all sorts of other strange things. Ocean sat on the bed while Sage dug through piles of stuff trying to find trousers, and passing me boomerangs and broken helicopters and so on as he did so.

"Here they are! I knew I had a pair of jeans somewhere. They should fit too, and they're quite new. I just sling on the same pair every day so I forgot about them."

I dried myself off and started to put them on, stupidly chucking a bouncy ball to Ocean so that he lobbed it back cheerfully when I had both hands full pulling the jeans up by the waistband, and I instinctively tried to catch it, and fell *thud* on the floor with my legs tied together just above the knees and the ball hit me on the head.

After we'd stopped laughing, I realized I could hear Mouse saying urgently, *Are you all right?*

Then it came to me that she was downstairs and outside,

and must have heard the crash; but it proved we could communicate at a distance, as she'd always said we could.

I'm fine, I thought back to her. *I can hear you! Can you talk to Tom?*

I'll try, came back Mouse, *but he has to be listening.*

Sage then decided to show me around the house properly. I don't know how I hadn't noticed the paintings, or maybe you'd call them collages, but now I saw they were all over the place. We paused at the first lot, on the walls along the stairs. I could see what the egg cartons and wire were for now; they were sort of embedded under layers of paint.

"Mum does these," Sage explained.

Maybe all the colors she wore sort of drained her, because she had a real thing going with grays and browns. Not what you'd call lively—the sort of no-color of our classroom walls. Maybe that's why I hadn't noticed them.

"Oh," I said, and "Ah," as we looked at them in turn. It was kind of hard to know what to say. I couldn't figure out much—that might have been a person, was that a sky?

Just then, she turned up behind us. I felt I should say something, so I heard myself going, "Do they take a long time?"

This luckily didn't seem to be the wrong thing, as Sage's mum smiled in a misty kind of way, and said, no, not when the mood was on her; she could do one in only a few days. I looked surprised at this, because they looked like they took, at most, half an hour each, but she took my surprise the other way, and said, yes, it was amazing how much one could achieve when one had something to communicate.

Now this had me stumped, of course, because I couldn't for the life of me see what the pictures were on about, other than general gloom, so I said, "Do they have titles?" hoping I might get a clue.

"Some of them do; mostly I change my mind after a while and call them something else. This one was called *Nothingness* originally, but now—well, I'm not sure." She waved a hand at a gray canvas with lumps and a few streaks.

"I think that's a fine title," I said, wondering how the heck anyone else was supposed to know what the picture was of, if even *she* didn't know.

Again, I seemed to have said the right thing, because she smiled and said, "Well, that's what I'll call it again, if you really think so." She was going to hang them soon in an exhibition, she said, so she'd have to come up with a title for all of them by then.

"Do you sell them?" I asked.

Her face clouded for a moment. They would be up for sale, of course, but the main point of an exhibition was *sharing* one's talent with the audience. She didn't like to sell them, she said; they were all like babies, to her. It hurt to part with them after all the work. And of course, art was so difficult to sell nowadays. Sensitive people, she said, had been moved to tears by her paintings; indeed, she'd actually had to take them down from a unit for depressed people where she'd had them on display, because the patients had so tuned in to the emotion in the paintings, it had just been too much for them.

"Ah," I said again, and nodded and rubbed my chin as if I had a beard, which was what Mr. Willis, one of our teachers at school, did when he was being wise about something.

That seemed to work all right, and we managed to get past the rest of the pictures and down the stairs, and now the strange boiled-plant smell was explained too.

"Oh!" she said suddenly, clapping her hand to her chest. "Didn't Chiffon say you had a *dog*? That rescued Bonzo? You *haven't* left it outside all this time?"

"Well, I . . ."

"*Do* bring it in, poor thing. I'm mostly a healer, thank

goodness—art sales being what they are. I make up own herbal remedies. I do animals too."

Mouse, I warned silently, as I headed for the kitchen and the back door to let her in, *be nice. She says she's a healer and she does animals.*

Does animals? I don't need healing. I will be nice—but she'd better not be like a vet.

I think she's harmless enough, just a bit wacky. She called you "it," by the way.

Mouse trotted in, looking a bit wary, but Sage's mum was delighted.

"Isn't it—he or she?—gorgeous?" she cried, reaching down and stroking Mouse's head.

"She," I said helpfully.

I can tell she's a natural, said Mouse. *It's just a bit worrying she doesn't know the difference between a male and a female. . . .*

"Let me see. Bring it—her—into the lounge and I'll check her out. It's the least I can do," she said, sweeping out of the kitchen.

Sage followed, looking not-very-interested. Ocean, I noticed, had disappeared.

The least she can do, said Mouse, trotting after her, *is give us dinner. And maybe a room for the night. Get on to it, kid.*

In the lounge, Sage's mum asked Sage to pull the curtains shut, and lit some little candles. They smelled pretty strong, a bit like the flowers you have for funerals. I felt the roof of my mouth coat with waxy smoke. It was worse for poor Mouse, of course, with her sensitive nose. She panted a bit, and only sneezed once, so she was trying her best to be polite.

Sage's mum dangled what looked like a bit of plastic or glass on the end of a cord over Mouse's back and closed her eyes.

"What's that?" I hissed to Sage.

"Crystal. Does something with energies, she says," he whispered back, doubtfully.

"Does it work?" I asked.

"Well, lots of people come to her and pay well for it, along with the remedies and so on. Most don't come back, but that's because they get better, Mum says."

"Have you had it done?" I whispered back.

"Only for her to practice. The remedies—I never notice any difference. The only medicine I ever had which worked so's you'd notice was antibiotics from the doctor. But Mum says they're bad for you."

"Oh," I said. "My brother's sick and he will have to take

medicine which might make him better but will als[o be]
bad for him. I wondered if your mum . . ."

Then we went quiet because Sage's mum was doing
weird kind of chanting, and pressing Mouse's back and
shoulders with her hands.

How's it feel, Mouse? I thought across to her as she stood
patiently.

OK, she said. *Like someone grooming you.*

Sage's mum stopped chanting, which was good, because
I found it a bit embarrassing, to be honest, and sat back on
her heels.

Sage took this to mean it was the end of the session, I
suppose, because he got up and drew the curtains back
again. It was starting to get dark.

"Well," said Sage's mum, looking serious, "that should
be better. She has a lot of bad energy around here"—waving
her hand over Mouse's shoulders—"which was giving her
some pain . . ."

No I haven't, and it wasn't, said Mouse, sitting down
calmly.

". . . but it should be fine now."

Oh for heaven's sake, said Mouse, getting up and starting
to sniff around.

hank you so much," I said, deciding to try a risky
tegy, "but we really should get back to Gran's now. She
ll wonder where we are. Dad is due to come over and
pick me up from there, you see."

Dad? Where did that come from? I wondered.

"Oh!" said Sage, looking disappointed. "Can't you stay
for dinner? We haven't done anything yet."

"Well, I—well, that would be great," I said, trying to
look surprised. "I'll have to give Gran a ring, if that would
be all right?"

I felt a stab of guilt about the last lie: pretending to be
a caring child when all this time everyone at home must
be worried sick because I hadn't phoned at all.

Listen, said Mouse, staring at me fixedly. *Say you wouldn't
eat till late anyway because your dad has to come all the way
from Tawntown to get you. You'll have to check he won't mind
coming out late.*

I wondered what she was playing at, but repeated her
words almost exactly.

She was a genius, of course.

"Tawntown!" said Sage's mum. "Oh, that is a way for
him, late in the evening." Then—"*I know!*"

She's got it, said Mouse.

"I have to go into Tawntown in the morning in any

case. Why don't you have dinner here and sleep
Then I can run you in with me! Oh, as long as your g
won't miss you . . ." She waited, eager as a child, delighte
with her idea. Sage turned big, green, hopeful eyes on me.

"No, no, Gran won't mind. I wasn't going to spend the
night at hers anyway. Well, that would be great if you're
sure it's no trouble? Dad would be pleased. . . ." Sage let
out a whoop.

"I'd better just ring him to stop him from setting out,"
I said, and Sage led me to the phone, where, luckily, he
left me to get on with it while he ran to tell Ocean.

Talking to a made-up dad when yours is dead, with the
call not really dialed, is a very strange experience. I
pushed the picture of my own dad back down, surprised it
had sprung up. I hardly ever thought of him anymore.
While I was saying, "So is that all right? And you'll tell
Gran? Oh great, thanks a lot. See you tomorrow . . ." I was
asking Mouse in our silent talk: *How did you know to say
Tawntown? And how did you know she'd offer to have us stay
and give us a lift?*

*I heard her agreeing to see someone, a client in Tawntown,
on the phone when you were upstairs with the boys. It's a good
way away, isn't it, in the direction we want? It was written big
and dark on the map.*

, I replied silently. *I looked at the towns enough on the* ₁. *I should have remembered. But I'm feeling a bit worried* ₍out *Tom, and Mum and Gran. All hell must be breaking* ₍oose *by now. I didn't come back from lunch with Michael, and I haven't phoned them.*

Mouse nudged my hand.

Don't forget my dinner, in your bag. Didn't I tell you, I talked to Tom already? You're safe for now, he told them you'd phoned and asked to sleep over at Michael's and they fell for it. But it'll only buy you till tomorrow afternoon at the latest.

That's something, at least, I thought back. *It's brilliant you got through to Tom. How is he?*

Not good, said Mouse, honestly, *but holding on.*

SIX
Sugar Pills and Water

After the pretend phone call, I felt a bit less wired up. I hadn't realized how the worry of the journey, getting somewhere for us to sleep, feeling guilty about Mum and Tom and Gran at home, Tom's health, the future meeting with Uncle David—how it had all weighed me down like a ton of bricks. Just for a while, I played with Sage, Ocean, and even Shiff like a proper kid again, and we had a lot of fun.

I gave Mouse her dinner in the kitchen, and no one seemed to notice or think it was odd I was carrying a bag around with dog food in it when I was visiting my gran for the day. Then we sat down to dinner, quite tired out, and it was piles of steaming stew—vegetarian, they told me—I couldn't tell you what was in it, but it tasted fine to me. With all the warmth and fullness in my stomach and after such a long day, I flopped down in a chair in front of the television with everyone else and my eyes started to close.

But later that evening, something a bit unpleasant happened.

We were watching a program about wolves, and I don't

think anyone was really that excited about it, but nothing else was on and no one could be bothered to change the channel. I was trying to get Mouse interested by telling her they were her distant relatives, but she was flopped out on the floor, and said she knew what her mum looked like, if not her dad, and these creatures (she seemed to think them a much lower form of life) certainly weren't relatives of hers. Before I could get into an argument with her, and just at an interesting moment, when the wolves might or might not catch a big deer, there was a ring at the doorbell, and Sage's mum went to answer it.

We heard her say, "Why, hello, Mr. Green, is anything the matter? Is it Sylvia?"

Then a man's voice, low at first but very angry, and getting louder.

"Well, yes, something is the matter. Sylvia died at four o'clock this afternoon."

We heard Sage's mum sounding a bit shocked, starting to say how sorry she was, but as we got to the lounge door to peep round and listen in, the man interrupted her.

"Sorry? *Sorry?* I should say you should be. She might still be here now if she'd taken the proper medication like the doctors told her. But you said, *you said,* 'No, it's bad for you.' Instead, she gets meditation, and chanting, and

66

mumbo jumbo, and these 'natural drops' and thes̶
ral little pills' . . ."

His voice was rising to a bellow. We could just see
in the open front doorway; Sage's mum had her hands
her chest and had taken a step back. He was a little, old
ish man, and a red had risen to his face, which you could
tell was usually pale and grayish. Thin scraps of gray hair
were swept over his bald head, and his watery eyes, sunk
deep into bags and creases, glared out from behind a pair
of spectacles. From somewhere deep in the scrawny frame,
draped in a respectable brown cardigan and suit trousers,
a giant monster, a great, dripping, club-wielding troll of
rage, was powering the voice which shook the walls of the
house.

Sage's mum tried faintly to interrupt again. "I can
only advise. Even in conventional medical circles, it's well
known it can go either way, in cases of . . . in cases such
as these. . . ."

"In cases of *cancer*, you mean?" he shouted. "There! I
can say it. Why can't you? There's no need to beat about
the bush. She's dead now, dead and gone and I am alone,
after *forty-five years*."

His voice broke for a moment, and his puny shoulders
sagged punier still beneath the cardigan. My heart pulled

udden terrible pain. I knew about death. But when
lost my dad, I was not old and alone and without
eone I had loved for forty-five years.

Sage's mum kept quiet. The old man pulled himself together a little, lowering his cracking voice, trying to control it.

"She did have a chance, with the proper medication. It
wasn't definitely terminal. There was at least a chance. I
showed the doctor what you gave her. *Do you know what
he told me?*" He thrust his face toward Sage's mum, and
now we could see in the light falling from the doorway,
over the dry creased desert of his skin, little rivulets of water were running.

Sage's mum seemed frozen, made no answer, as she
knew he asked for none.

"For cancer, and for fifty pounds a consultation, that
medicine you gave her, *do you know what he told me it
was?*"—again, the silence in the pause, heavy as a killing
blanket of snow over the bodies of lambs—"Sugar pills
and water."

He staggered back out of the doorway.

"Sugar pills and water! Nothing, nothing in it at all but
sugar and water! To kill cancer, goddammit, to kill cancer,
to save my wife." And his voice broke again and he reeled

away as if drunk, away into the dark, and we couldn't ·
him anymore, but we could hear him, crying softly, grow
ing fainter.

Sage's mum vaguely held out an arm as he disappeared,
but then dropped it by her side.

After a moment, she closed the door, stood still facing it.

Then she took a breath, turned around, and saw us.

"Well. Poor Sylvia. Poor Mr. Green," and shaking her
head, she came back into the lounge, sat down on the
sofa again, and patted the cushion next to her for Shiff to
join her.

"A terrible thing, grief. He will rail at the world, and
everyone will be to blame for a while," she said, reaching
for the television control. "Now, is anything else on, I
wonder?"

Shiff and Ocean, I noticed, started to glue their eyes to
the screen again, but I looked across at Sage as I clam-
bered back into my armchair and saw him staring into
space, distracted.

Mouse, who had stood behind us all at the doorway
during the shouting, in case she might be needed for de-
fense, settled down again; but her eyes were restless, her
ears at half-tilt, listening.

I can still hear him, even if you can't, she said. *On and on, ugar pills and water," he howls, he cries. This is bad. Oh, this is bad.*

Will he be all right? I thought over to her, as canned laughter played to a not-very-funny comedy show.

He is old, it is not just the fact that he has lost her which causes him to pine, it is the way in which he lost her. Maybe it need not have happened, someone is to blame, he needs revenge, but he will not take it, he seeks justice, but he will not find it. Unless he can grieve and accept and then go on with his life, I am afraid he will pine and die. It may not happen immediately, but it will happen, and it will all be down to this loss.

I pleaded tiredness and a headache, and went off to bed just afterward. Sage came up and lent me a pair of pajamas. We didn't talk about Mr. Green, but it was there, between us. I could tell that Sage felt bad about his mum, especially it all happening in front of me, who he liked; I felt bad that he felt bad, and also because now I knew there was nothing in this place which could do Tom any good. Just for a moment it felt like there might have been a strand, a spiderweb silk of hope, but Mr. Green's speech had taken a great pair of shears and just chopped straight through it.

Sage had dug out a camping mat and cleared a space for me on his floor. By the time I was getting into Sage's sleeping bag, truly tired, he looked really miserable.

"It's just, she's not very good at anything," he said, brushing away a tear and standing motionless at the door.

I tried to think of something to say. "Don't say that. One of our teachers, Mr. Willis, he says never say that about anyone. He would say she just hasn't found what she's good at yet."

"Mmm," said Sage, sadly, "maybe that's true. I wonder what it is?"

"You'll have to have a think," I said, growing sleepy, "and then maybe steer her a bit that way. Get her to try rock climbing. Flower arranging. Fixing cars. Mr. Willis says, how many people might there be who could have been specially designed to be world-champion, Olympic-standard skiers or rowers or boxers or whatever you can think of, but who've never tried it?"

Sage managed a little giggle.

"She might be a bit old for that by now. But there must be something. I suppose just anything but painting and healing."

"Anything but that," I agreed.

That night I slept restlessly, dreaming Tom's dreams. Tom was pushing through what seemed to be a crowded station, looking for something. There was a Wanted poster with an ordinary-looking man's face on it, and KILLER written underneath. Through people's rushing legs, he saw a dog—a bit like Mouse, but it wasn't her. That was it, he was looking for Mouse. He had lost her, in all those people. And then there was the man from the poster, staring at him. The feeling of panic, then of trying to ignore the figure, of trying not to give away that he had recognized him. More dogs passing between people—surely that was Mouse? But always when the dog was close, it changed color or had the wrong fur; it was never her. And always the terrifying feeling, as he slipped among the crowds, that the wanted killer was following, hunting. Desperation and horror rose in my chest, until it woke me, sweating and shaking.

The next morning, Sage's mum was up and about as if nothing had happened, and after breakfast, I said goodbye to Sage, Shiff, and Ocean, and Mouse licked Bonzo for Shiff, because she insisted, and we all shrieked about germs, and I wrote down their address so that I could write and say thank you, though I am not very good at that sort of thing, and I got in the car with Sage's mum, who reminded Sage not to drown Shiff while she was out, and Mouse got in the back, and we set off for Tawntown.

SEVEN
Freaky Mad

I had to think pretty sharp in the car. I had no address in Tawntown. I thought of suggesting a place in the middle of town like the High Street—there was bound to be a High Street, wasn't there?—where I was meeting the pretend dad. But when I put this idea past Mouse, she said Sage's mum would then be more likely to hang around to meet him, as it was a bit of a crowded place to leave a kid.

I don't think a big town or city is a good place for us, said Mouse. *More human people, more danger. Let's stick to the countryside. We might have to walk from now on.*

Then I thought of how I'd had a lift in other kids' parents' cars—you'd often point and say, "Oh here it is—just here." I decided to try it.

We drove on through villages and empty sunlit roads with green, soft, rolling countryside and farms. Some of the cottages even had roofs made of thatch. They looked big and comfortable and heavy, as if they were squashing the little old building underneath. It looked like pictures out of books, places you saw on telly. They didn't have our mountains, but I liked it all right—it looked a bit cozier than our wildness up north.

When we'd been driving for the best part of an hour, and I noticed more and more signs to Tawntown, I started to look out for likely houses, still out in the countryside.

"Oh," I said cheerfully, "I think we're coming in on our road. Yes!"

"Oh!" said Sage's mum. "You live out here. That's nice. And how handy for me. Where do I go?"

I saw a few houses scattered ahead.

"Just on this road, you don't have to turn off." And I craned forward from the backseat as if looking for my own house.

"That's it, coming up," I said, fixing on one which wasn't too big and wasn't too small. "The brown one with the big chimney."

Sage's mum signaled and pulled over to the side of the road.

"Thanks, thanks so much," I said hastily, grabbing my bag and climbing out. I let Mouse out of the back door.

"No problem. Thank you. And do keep in touch!" And with a cheery wave, she was off.

I let out my breath with a sigh of relief as I waved back.

Not very responsible, said Mouse. *She should have checked you got in the door all right.*

"But lucky for us she's not like that," I said.

Right, said Mouse, *unless something turns up, we'll be walking from now on. This looks like a footpath and it leads through those woods and in the right direction, south. Shall we get going?*

The footpath ran between straggly hedges in the gap made by two of the houses. We set off along it, but I was worrying about how long the walking would take.

"I wonder how far it is in miles from here to Uncle David's," I said after a while, as we were approaching trees, "and how long that will take us to walk. I'm only covered at home until about lunchtime."

Ah, said Mouse, pausing to sniff. *As far as time goes, we aren't going to make it in a day on foot; and as far as being covered till lunchtime goes, I did manage to chat a bit with Tom while we were in the car. Unfortunately, Michael's mum came into the shop first thing this morning.*

"Oh dear," I said, stopping suddenly.

Yes, well, there was a brief conversation between your mum and Michael's, and Tom felt the shock waves back at home very shortly afterward, from what I can gather. Keep walking, keep walking. After what I've said about time, you won't make anything better by standing there.

I gave myself a shake and followed Mouse beneath the shade of the trees. I tried to think. The ground was soft and muffled my footfalls. A small bird darted silently away on one side.

"What did Tom tell them?" I asked.

He told them you were safe, just delivering me somewhere, and would be in contact and back very soon. Then he went off to sleep, and they couldn't exactly interrogate him.

"I suppose I must phone them, but I don't know what I'd say . . . ," I began.

You mean, you don't want to phone them because they'll shout at you, corrected Mouse, calmly.

"Shout at me, yes, OK—but if they maybe start crying or something . . . ugh . . ." I shuddered. "It makes me feel guilty if I don't phone but I'll feel even guiltier if I do."

Well, let's see how the day goes, and it might not be long— began Mouse, but broke off suddenly and stood still in front of me on the path.

"What is it?" I asked. Her nose twitched from side to side, her ears were in the up position, and her eyes were wary.

Dog, she said, and then we both saw it, trotting toward us on the path ahead.

It was a big, male yellow Labrador, marking his territory, hurrying on again. He didn't seem to have noticed us yet.

"What's the problem?" I asked Mouse. "Carry on. If we meet the owner, I'm just walking my dog."

There's something funny about him, said Mouse, stock-still, her fur starting to rise on her back.

I looked at the dog again. He had a cocky way of going along, with his elbows stuck out and his toes turned in, and his tail held up rather stiff and high; but after all, it *was* just a Labrador.

At that moment, a bit late in the day because he'd been busy sniffing and marking, he saw us.

He froze for a minute, staring, then something in his deep brown eyes changed—I swear they became lighter—and he hurtled toward us, making a sound of tearing cloth as he came.

Get out of here! I'LL TEAR YOUR HEAD OFF! he screamed.

I stood still in shock, and Mouse—who was first in the firing line—to give her credit, didn't move a muscle.

He thundered up to Mouse, snarling and ripping at air, foam flying from his lips, all his words running into one: *I'LL TEAR YOUR HEAD OFF I'LL TEAR YOUR HEAD OFF I'LL TEAR YOUR HEAD OFF!*

He came to a screeching halt in front of Mouse; the terrible lines which had drawn his face into a mask of hate suddenly dropped away, the floppy jowls and ears hung down, and he wagged his tail.

Hi there! Pleased to meet you!

"*Shoooooot*, that's not funny!" I said to Mouse. "That was too scary! I thought—"

Shhh, said Mouse. *Something's not right.*

The Labrador circled us, sniffed, wagging his tail. Mouse tried a gentle wag, but in a flash, he was off again, foaming lips pulled back over teeth, a ridge of fur high on his back.

I'LL TEAR YOUR HEAD OFF! I'LL TEAR YOUR HEAD OFF!

And this time he went for her, but Mouse, ready, sprang for his neck. Only half his size, and less than half his weight, suddenly she looked small. I had never seen her beaten—she didn't pick fights but occasionally had to defend herself—but now I stepped forward, really worried. The big dog missed with his jaws but knocked Mouse over

78

on her back; there was a flurry of snarling, then suddenly the two were circling again.

Mouse was calm and slow with apparently no anger; the yellow dog was all puppy-faced again and wagging his tail: *Pleased to meet you, pleased to meet you!*

Now we go on our way, not rushing, said Mouse. *Just see if we can get past. Where the heck is this nutter's owner?*

At that moment, there was the sound of someone tripping over a root, and a muffled curse, and a boy appeared, looking cross.

"Barney! Get here!"

He was about thirteen or fourteen, I would say, with brownish hair cut quite short, and he had a leash in his hand.

He hardly glanced at us.

Barney skulked up to him and the boy attached the leash. Then he looked over at me, and I realized he was embarrassed.

"I'm sorry, his bark's worse than his bite."

"No damage," I said cheerfully.

Only to his brain, sniffed Mouse, looking at Barney disdainfully.

The boy smiled at us.

"To tell you the truth, I don't meet many—or any—other

79

kids walking dogs here. So I thought you were bound to be an old lady or something! I mean, can you imagine?"

I smiled back.

"Would he *eat* one of those little dogs they have?" I asked.

"Oh, no, he wouldn't hurt a fly. Well, I don't reckon," he added rather vaguely. "You new here?"

"No, I'm on a really big walk," I told him, on the spur of the moment. "Holidays and all. School's planning some award we can take part in, but we have to do a twenty-five-mile walk for it. Thought I'd get some practice in."

"What a bore for you," he drawled, flicking Barney's ear. "Glad *my* school isn't doing that. Do you *have* to do it?"

"Well, no, but they sort of expect it," I made up frantically, then added with a stroke of genius, "And anyway, we get to miss lessons. Loads of lessons."

"Oh, well, then, I suppose even I'd do it in that case. Lucky you. Which way are you going?"

This way, said Mouse. *The direction in which we are pointing.*

"Just through the woods here. I'm sort of heading south generally on a compass bearing. I'll go as far as I can and then call for a lift, I reckon."

"Come back to mine instead, I'm bored as hell. I bet I

80

can get Dad to give you a lift and then you can tell whoever it is that you've done your practice."

The boy had an odd way of thinking, to my mind, because if I was really doing a practice run for a massive
walk, I'd be no fitter if I cheated—but I leaped at the idea
of another lift.

"OK, thanks," I said. "I'm John and this is Mouse."

"Pete," he said. "You met Barney—I'll keep him on the
leash. I'd just keep Mouse away from him if I were you."

"I think she's got that," I said, and we set off back the
way we'd already come.

*I'm with you on this so far, because of the lift, and because
it's a kid,* warned Mouse, *but the dog is freaky mad. Bear in
mind someone or something made him like that.*

We followed Pete off the path as we came toward the
road, and along the edge of a field. Then left down a
rough track running alongside a railed paddock, full of
lush grass. Next there was a smaller paddock, pretty bare
of grass, with a set of shabby timber stables in it, and three
small ponies mooching about.

I could see a big garden beyond, full of tall, dark evergreens which loomed over the mossy lawn and seemed to
have menaced all flowers from the borders. You could just
see a glimpse of a house between the great branches.

"Is this yours, then?" I asked, impressed.

"Yep," said Pete, pausing because I had stopped.

"And the paddocks? The ponies?"

"Yep."

"Wow." I was about to ask if he rode, but the ponies were very small. "Does someone ride, then?"

"No, no, they're Dad's. He's a scientist."

He was happy enough to wait while I admired the ponies, though I could tell he wasn't very interested in them himself. I didn't get why a scientist wanted little ponies, but I didn't want to seem stupid, so I stroked the one that had come over to investigate. She had very dark brown hair like a chestnut, deepening to almost black in parts, and a beige nose and rings round her eyes. Her blue-black hooves looked impossibly tiny beneath her stocky body.

Nice horses, said Mouse, sniffing at the pony's nose.

If you were a wolf, you'd eat them, I teased her.

Then this is more proof that I am not *related to wolves*, said Mouse smugly.

We carried on to the house, and followed Pete in through a side door of a low building which I took to be a garage, attached to one side.

It *was* a garage of sorts, I realized when we were inside;

it was bare and made of concrete, and there was a large and shiny silver car parked at the far end of it. But what grabbed you straightaway were the rows and rows of wire-mesh cages along both walls. Mouse stopped and her fur prickled up.

Don't like it, was all she said.

They were empty and cobwebby, and while I looked at them in surprise, Pete calmly opened the door of a large one at floor level and bundled Barney inside.

He saw me looking.

"Dad used to keep rabbits and rats and so on here. He doesn't use them anymore. But this one's still Barney's."

Still Barney's? said Mouse. *Don't think for a minute I'm going in one of those.*

"Wow," I said again, knowing Pete was the kind of kid who lived off people being impressed by his stuff, even if it was really his dad's stuff, "how cool. Mouse will be all right just in here or the garden, won't she? I'm afraid she's not used to a cage."

"Yeah, wherever," said Pete, "as long as it's not in the house. Dad won't have animals in the house."

"Why doesn't he keep animals here anymore?" I asked, peering into a dark and dusty cage.

"Doesn't need them. Says he's done enough with

83

vermin. The ponies are the thing now," he continued cheerfully. "Reckons they're going to make our fortune."

I hate this place, said Mouse. *It stinks of the vet's.*

It's only cleaning chemicals and antiseptic, I expect, I silently reassured her.

It's that, and the chemicals given out from animals in terror and death, snapped Mouse irritably. *Leave the scent analysis to me. I have superior equipment, remember?*

OK, OK, I'm sorry. I'll leave the door open so you can get out into the garden, I thought across to her, *but see if you can get anything out of Barney that might be useful.*

It's worth a try, but I really think he's a bit beyond hope, said Mouse. *The boy's locked that cage properly, hasn't he?*

Yes, I said. *Keep in touch.* I slipped my bag from my back and left it near the door to the garden, and followed Pete in through another door, next to Barney's cage.

We stepped into a large hall, with dark wooden floors and a smell of polish. The walls were tall and painted dull colors, and there were grand plaster curls and twirls and decoration everywhere—where the walls met the ceilings, round the pretend chandeliers. There was a big plant in a dark corner and I couldn't think how it grew with no light, but I touched it as we passed and felt dusty plastic.

Pete pushed open another door, this time into a large

kitchen. I gasped as I stepped into the room. It was like being inside an advertisement. There was shiny steel and a kind of black marble effect and something space-age, which might have been a sink, where a man was standing with a kettle in his hand.

He was medium-sized, and looked older than I'd expected, his hair nearly white, short and neat like Pete's. He was filling the kettle. Now he said jokily, "Why, Pete, what've you got there?" which I didn't think was very polite, to be honest.

Pete explained who I was—or rather, who I'd said I was—and what I said I was doing, and threw in the bit about the lift, I noticed gratefully.

Pete's dad seemed to be looking at me rather too closely for my liking, measuring me up, all the time Pete was talking. But when Pete was done, he said, "Good to hear kids are walking again. Lose their legs soon, I've told Pete. That's why he was out with Barney. I can give you a lift later, maybe. Do you want a cup of tea? I was just putting on the kettle."

He had a strange way of only moving his mouth when he was talking, while the rest of his face stayed frozen still, but I put away thoughts of a killer robot in a dad disguise and said yes to the tea, not because I wanted it, but

85

because I knew that it was sensible to take all food and drink offered in case I went without later.

As he got on with making the tea and Pete hauled himself up on the counter and swung his legs, I said, "This is some kitchen. My mum would love this."

"Ah," said Pete's dad, stirring the tea. "Sadly, Pete's mum no longer lives with us. Just us boys to appreciate it." He put the teapot lid on carefully and started to get cups out. "Mind you, I admit I don't get time to cook much nowadays. Too busy working."

"Pete said you were a scientist," I said, sitting down in a chrome-and-leather chair at the counter next to Pete, as it didn't seem right to copy him, "and you're studying ponies."

He was waiting for the tea to brew. He looked at me, maybe a touch warily.

"Why, yes, that's right. Takes a lot of time, a lot of work."

"I think it sounds great. I might like to do that one day," I said.

Pete's dad lost the wary look.

"Really? You good at science?"

Before I could answer, he was talking, his eyes lit up. You could tell this was about him, not about me, so I didn't have to say anything much.

"Let me tell you, science can be rewarding—very rewarding—but"—here his eyes narrowed sharply, and did they, like Barney's, go a little lighter?—"it can also be an ungrateful master. I worked hard—very hard—for years, and came out with, pah, nothing—bar this house. . . ."

I thought of the house, the kitchen, the big car, the paddocks, ponies. I looked over at Pete. He was looking faintly bored.

"But I do think I'll crack it on my own this time with these ponies, and then we'll see, won't we?" He actually rubbed his hands together, and smiled across at Pete.

Pete smiled back, a bit dutifully I thought. "Tea will be ready by now, Dad," he reminded, swinging his heels against the cupboard door below.

"Oh yes." Pete's dad turned and poured us a cup each. He didn't add sugar and I didn't dare ask if they had any. I said thank you and took a gulp. It was hot and bitter.

"But it's not just about money," he continued, looking past me and into some world of his own, "it's about respect. Reaching the heights . . ."

And having everyone look up to you, I thought to myself. I get it.

"Is it top-secret?" I asked, sounding like an impressed little kid. "Your discovery, or whatever it is?"

"No, no—well, I've yet to perfect it, in any case. It's to do with obesity."

"Obesity?" I was surprised. What had ponies got to do with fat people?

He looked pleased that he'd hooked my interest.

"It's my theory that a lot of people are, as has often been argued, not really fat through their own overeating, but through genes."

I nodded to show I understood.

"I think, like the wild native ponies, obese people were designed to live in places where food wasn't abundant all year round, and work was very hard. You had to eat a lot of food when it was available, otherwise you'd starve when there was none."

"And now," I said, "with less tough work, and supermarkets . . ."

Pete's dad nodded eagerly and continued: "And ways of storing food like refrigerators and so on, these people are not able to switch off the 'eat while it's here' signal from their genes. And they just get fat."

"And is that what you're doing? Working out how to switch off that signal?" I asked eagerly. It sounded great. Those poor people would be relieved.

"Well, kind of," said Pete's dad, suddenly vague, "though

it's not that simple. One thing is for sure, though. The amount of money spent on obesity, on treatment, dieting— it's a gold mine, the whole area." He tipped the dregs of his cup into the sink, and Pete jumped off the counter.

"Come on, John," he said. "My computers are upstairs."

"You'll have to come and remind me about that lift," warned Pete's dad. "I'll be working in my study if you want me. I lose track of time."

"OK. Thanks for the tea," I said to Pete's dad, and followed Pete to his room.

It soon became clear that the way into Pete's confidence, like I'd guessed, was generally to admire and flatter. It also helped that I just wasn't as good as him at computer games; I didn't have to pretend that.

Pete had not one, but two computers and various consoles, joysticks, and all sorts of extras, in a surprisingly tidy room.

I obediently battled and slogged through screens of blood and gore for a while, but eventually started to give up and watch Pete, which was kind of boring but easier, and Pete seemed as happy with me doing that as trying to compete against him, after he'd beaten me hollow a few times.

I didn't really know why, because I should have been

concentrating on my journey to Uncle David's and worrying about the family back at home, but I had this thirst to know about Barney and the ponies. Something was nudging at me. I didn't know what it was, but it was that same kind of feeling you get if you walk past a kid being bullied at school. The something says, "Are you going to do anything? Should you? What are you going to do?"

"Barney'd like this game," I joked to him. "Maybe they should do one with dogs in it for him."

Pete chuckled.

"Yeah. Mind you, he should attack people, really, not dogs. I mean, that was supposed to be what he was trained for."

"People? You mean, he should have gone for me, instead of Mouse?"

I couldn't help thinking of Pete's joke about little old ladies. What if Barney had met one of those?

"Well, no, of course not. Not if the training worked properly. Only on command, or burglars."

But the training *hadn't* worked properly, had it? Which meant, who knew *what* Barney would decide was a target. I thought Pete should really keep Barney on a leash, and maybe muzzled, but I decided not to say anything, as I wanted to keep him talking.

"Did your dad train him?" I tried.

"Yeah, trying some new method he worked out using electric shocks. Can't say I'm too impressed so far. Course, might be because he's a Lab. A German shepherd or Doberman would have been the thing, but Dad doesn't like paying for animals, and Barney was the only free dog he could get."

"Ah," I said. "Well, your dad is one clever guy. I bet your friends are jealous, with you having a dad like that, and this nice house and everything."

Sometimes, I'm ashamed of myself, I admit. But you know that moment when you say just the right thing to get out of someone what you want? This was that moment.

Pete took his eyes off the screen for a fraction of a second to glance at me.

"You know, I never thought of that, of them being jealous. Yeah, I bet you're right; I bet that's it." He tilted his chin out proud and blasted an alien blob monster to pieces.

"Ooh, well hit!" I said, then, all innocent: "What do you mean? Do some of them have a go at you?"

There was a pause in the game as he'd reached a new level.

"Me and Dad, we've learned to keep a bit quiet about the animal side of things. There are some nutters around who think it's better for people to die of diseases than for something way down the food chain to even break a claw. Rats and rabbits—vermin! People have to kill 'em every day. Trouble with kids, they have pets—they can't see the difference. But I bet you're right. They are just jealous because they have crummier houses and live in horrible places. Dad said that's what brought him down—spite and jealousy."

"Brought him down?" I said, remembering Pete's dad saying science was ungrateful and that he'd "come out" without much. I wanted to know more.

It all flooded out now. It's often the way with quiet, grumpy people, isn't it? You hit the nail on the head and it just spills out. You don't have to say anything else—in fact, you might as well not be there. Take now, for example—Pete had that light in his eyes, like he was on his favorite topic, and he was really looking just past me, at the wall.

"He was well paid, working in a laboratory for a big company. Then they fired him—*they* said, for breaches of animal welfare. He couldn't understand it. What the heck does it matter how you treat something that's just going to get killed at the end of the experiment anyway? He reckoned it was because he was so good, and the guy in charge was frightened that one day Dad'd get his job."

So he wasn't even a really top scientist, I thought—someone else was in charge.

"And then, well, someone leaked something to the papers—spite again, I guess—and Mum left around that time, and we had to move out of that area. . . ."

Pete looked down at the carpet, and I had to admit, I felt a bit sorry for him. His dad might have turned him into his own mouthpiece and a pretty unpleasant person, but you could see the picture all right. He was lonely and isolated. And he didn't seem to have made any real friends here, either.

"But he's on the edge of a breakthrough," I prompted, as if to cheer him up.

"Yeah, that's right!" His eyes lit up again. He leaned toward me and gave a little giggle. It didn't make me want to giggle back. I wondered if he wasn't a bit—well, loose in the head, if you know what I mean. I did my best to make my face look encouraging.

"The obesity thing. When this diet pill is marketed—we'll be rich forever!" He sat back in his chair for a moment, with a rather smug expression.

"And he's made the pill?" I asked.

"Well, no, though he's working on that. Something went wrong and the whole first lot of ponies had to be shot." Pete sighed. "When the native ponies get fat on too much really good grass—stuff they're not designed to eat, where they come from—they get a sickness called laminitis. Their feet get hot and they can't walk. It's hard to cure and if it's left, their hooves actually start to fall off and the bone inside can turn round. That's what happened with that batch."

"Oh dear," I said.

"Yes, Dad was cross. We don't have a lot of money coming in as yet, and it was a heck of a waste, though they were cheap. That's why he got this lot free. You can just get them off the moor, they're wild. Anyway, he thinks he might get it right this time; he's almost sure. He lets them onto the rich grass tomorrow."

Some people just don't stop socking you in the face with surprises, do they? I couldn't get over the way Pete thought that when I said "Oh dear" about the poor ponies, I was just thinking of the money thing, like him and his dad.

When he talked about his dad's plan to get rich, Pete's eyes definitely went kind of creepy—something he shared with his dad, and even Barney. I felt my skin start to crawl. There seemed to be a kind of background electricity in this house, a static, like before a storm or walking under humming power lines. I remembered Mouse's doubts when we'd followed Pete back here. But if I went pale or anything, Pete didn't seem to notice.

I managed a shaky smile. "But—if he's not totally sure the pill will work, won't these ponies end up like the first lot?"

"Well, to be honest, it's quite likely," said Pete, nodding, and I saw a flicker of doubt in his eyes as he looked back to the computer screen for a moment. "But, as they say, you can't make an omelette without breaking eggs. Anyway, they didn't cost anything."

I swallowed. The feeling of building static seemed to crackle under my skin, to reach the inside of my skull. My teeth hummed with it. I wanted to get out of here, right now. Fast.

On the other hand, I needed the lift. Most likely, everything would be fine and Mouse and I would be well on the way to Uncle David's by nightfall and I could finish this whole thing and phone Mum and Tom and . . .

You know what I said about that annoying pushing, prodding feeling, the one you get if you walk past the little kid getting bullied around at school? It's kind of in your stomach and then somewhere in your chest.

All of a sudden, I felt the soft breath of that pony I'd stopped and petted; warm, blowing on my hand, the tickling

95

of its whiskers, as real and clear as if it was happening right now, though I was sitting in Pete's room.

I liked ponies. Me and Tom used to climb on ones in Mr. Jones's field, because we hadn't a pony of our own, and we'd seen Wild West films. We'd been secretive about it, because we thought Mr. Jones might be cross, as they weren't ours to climb on. We didn't want to gallop about or worry them or anything. We'd have fallen off, in any case. We just wanted to see what it felt like.

It took us a while to get the ponies to trust us because, of course, they didn't have any halters or saddles or bridles on, so they had to agree to it, and I suppose it was kind of silly and we might have been hurt, but it was fine. We sat up there on their warm backs in the evening sun, and the midges danced around us, and the ponies just mooched on, grazing the grass, a step at a time, and after a while it would make us kind of mellow and we'd lie down on them, and hear the grind, grind of their teeth and I swear you could never be more content since when you were a baby in your mother's arms and she sang you off to sleep.

One day, Mr. Jones told Mum to tell us he'd known all along, and not to worry about him being cross, because we made the ponies so easy and gentle to train. We hadn't realized that no one had ridden them or had even sat on their backs before. But you can guess how annoyed and worried Mum was about it.

I couldn't just go on and leave these ponies to be turned out onto the rich grass tomorrow. Grass which would probably bring a terrible and painful death.

You know what it's like when you make the right decision but it's still going to be hard. I felt a kind of relief and a kind of gloom at the same time. I was going to save the ponies (relief) but it would hold up my journey (gloom); I didn't know how I was going to do it (gloom) and I might get caught (gloom).

Pete hadn't noticed my silence as I sat thinking. He was absorbed in his game. If I didn't act soon, Pete's dad would be offering me that lift. I asked where the bathroom was, and headed off through the house, ignoring the directions. I was ready to say I'd got lost if I was caught, but I didn't run into Pete's dad. Hopefully, he was too busy thinking up crackpot ideas in his study to worry about me.

Mouse, I thought as I headed for the side door in the hall which led to the garage, *quiet, now, but we have to get out of here. Will Barney bark if I come in?*

He's asleep. Be very quiet with the door handle. If you set him off, hide and I'll pretend it was my fault if someone comes to look.

Slowly I turned the handle. I had one eye looking over my shoulder for Pete or Pete's dad and an ear to the door to hear signs that Barney might be about to explode in his cage.

The door handle gave a slight squeak. I paused.

You're OK so far, encouraged Mouse. *He's out like a light. Come on.*

I gave a little extra turn and the door swung open. I was through it in a flash, and wanted to shut it as quickly in case someone came, but had to do it quietly, carefully, knowing I was just centimeters from Barney's cage door.

Mouse was standing just outside, motionless, but ears pricked and tail high.

I can't wait to get out of here, too. What's up?

Quietly, quietly, I picked up my bag from where I'd left it.

I'm sorry, Mouse, we had a lift offered. But I don't want to take it.

I was out of the garage now, and down the garden as quick as a flash, dodging behind the dark towers of the evergreens in case someone was looking from the house. Mouse hurtled ahead.

That's all right; I do not think these are trustworthy humans. Barney doesn't make much sense, but what I managed to get from him was terrible. He has been through such shock and pain . . . you can't imagine. She stopped to wait for me and I saw her give a little shudder.

"I think I can, actually. I can't do anything for Barney right now, but I can save the ponies."

We had come onto the path alongside the bare paddock.

What?

"I know, Mouse, but I can't just leave them. Tomorrow he will turn them out onto the rich grass and they will probably start to get a disease which—"

I understand, I understand, said Mouse. *Just undo the gate and let them go and we'll get cracking.*

"It's not that simple," I said. "You can't just let ponies loose. They'll run on the road and cause an accident, or get killed, or both. And there's a whole field of rich grass here. They'll just stop there and start eating that and get ill anyway."

Oh for goodness' sake, whoever heard of animals so silly they'd make themselves ill from eating? said Mouse, exasperated.

"You, for one—if someone left eight bags of dog food open, or a pile of chocolate. These ponies can't help it either—they stuff themselves on poor grass all day where they come from and never get ill. They don't know the rich grass is different."

Mouse looked a bit sheepish. *I wouldn't die, though, if I ate too much. You just throw up, don't you?*

"Ponies can't throw up, Mouse. Now, are you going to help?"

How? She wagged her tail despite herself. She did have a soft spot for ponies.

"Sneak in the stables and see if there are some bits of rope hanging up. We can lead them with those."

We? she said, and paused. *Isn't this stealing?*

"He took them off the moor. They were wild. They're not his. They're captured. That's different," I said, hoping I was right.

Disgusting, said Mouse. *I am surprised they are so obliging. Hold on, I'll fetch the rope things if there are any.* And she dashed away toward the stables.

I stood by the gate, out of sight of the house, and the ponies, bored by the lack of grass in their bare paddock, ambled over to me with pricked ears.

Besides the one which was chestnut-colored, with a black mane and tail (Mr. Jones had told us that color was called *bay* by horse people), there was a little white mare (which is called *gray*), and a dusty black mare with a velvet muzzle and very long mane and tail, who looked much older. While they bickered over who should have most attention—the black mare seemed to be the boss, putting her ears back and snapping at the others—Mouse had been at work and was running back, tripping slightly over the ropes hanging from her mouth.

"They aren't exactly wild. Luckily. Hope this means we get the halters on all right," I said to Mouse.

I hurried as much as I could, aware that at any moment Pete would come looking for me from the house, or worse, his dad. What would I say? Just taking the ponies for a walk?

I slipped the simple rope halters over their noses and behind their furry, short ears. At least these weren't webbing headcollars, with buckles and so on. Mr. Jones had shown me and Tom how to put these on, after our secret was out, but I wasn't very quick at it. Thankfully, lead ropes had been left clipped onto the halters.

I arranged two ropes in one hand and one, the black mare's, in the other, figuring she wouldn't be so cooperative if she was bunched up with another pony. I opened the gate with fear rising in my stomach. I'd never led three ponies before, and I knew that if they wanted to take off, I wasn't going to be able to stop them. But the main thing was not to let *them* know that. So I acted calm and talked softly, and they hurried out after me, looking as pleased as dogs being taken for a walk.

EIGHT
Pinching Ponies

Where to? asked Mouse, taking up a lead position.

"I just want to get out of sight, for a start," I said. I hadn't the faintest idea where I was taking the ponies, and the sick feeling of fear was getting worse, if anything. I was realizing it's one thing not to have a Plan B, for when Plan A goes wrong; but more scary still not even to have a Plan A.

We'd better not go back in the woods, said Mouse. *That's the first place they'll look and I don't think it leads anywhere useful, just back to where we came from.*

"Then we can only go further along this field edge, behind the last few houses, and see where it goes," I said. "Not very undercover, except for the hedge."

I think they'll miss you, eventually, but they can't see the ponies from the house easily. They might not notice they're missing for some time. The ponies can wander in and out of the stables, too, so they'll probably assume they're in there, even if they do see the paddock is empty. I know how humans think. They're not good searchers. Keep up.

Mouse trotted on, behind the paddock, across the field it was cut from, and back toward the hedge. But the three ponies yanked on the ropes and plunged their heads down into the sweet, long, green grass, desperate after being trapped for so long in the bare paddock nearby. I would manage to pull one up, but then another would be at it. When their heads were up, they would trot ahead, pulling me nearly off my feet, and then stop again and start eating.

I began to get hot and sweaty, and the skin of my hands was sore in no time from the dragging ropes.

"It's all right for you, telling me to keep up, Mouse," I complained.

She looked back as I hauled at the gray pony's rope and managed to get its head up, while the black mare trod on my heel because I'd stopped so quickly and the bay mare put *her* head down.

I felt close to crying with frustration.

Now, said Mouse, *we aren't going to get anywhere like this, are we? While we are in this grass, leave the two free and just lead the black one. She's the boss, they'll follow her—if you can keep her moving.*

It seemed dangerous to let two go loose, but I could see the sense of it, so I tied the ropes short so the ponies couldn't trip on them, and then I let them go. They started grazing immediately, but the black mare walked on, good as gold, as if she knew what I was doing. Then the younger two saw her traveling on with us and stopped eating and trotted to catch up.

And so we followed the field's edge like this, with the younger ponies only pausing to snatch a mouthful here and there.

At the corner of the field, we came to a gateway onto the road, and we steadied for a moment. I looked up and down the asphalt ribbon. It was flanked by old hedgerows and trees and didn't seem to have any houses along it for miles.

There, said Mouse, looking directly across from the open gateway. Opposite was a thin, earthy track running between trees and nettles, into what looked like a thicket. A weathered wooden sign pointed toward it, and I could just make out the words *Bridle Path.*

"That'll do," I said, but Mouse was already across the road and on her way. I grabbed all three ropes, not coping with the idea of the ponies being loose on the road. A quick glance for traffic, and I was hurrying the ponies across, hooves tapping, my heart thumping, and then we were onto muffled earth, and the trees closed around us.

A bend in the track meant that we were out of sight of the road in seconds.

Here we stopped for a moment, and I dropped the two younger ponies' ropes and let the old mare's rope out long enough for her to join them grazing the scrub grass at the edge of the path. I pulled my bag off my back and dragged out the crumpled map.

"I have to get them to the moors, where they came from," I told Mouse. "The moors are south, but a bit to the side of where we are heading. Out of our way."

If it's got to be done, it's got to be done, said Mouse. *It's a shame we are traveling in daylight, though. Me and you sneaking about is one thing, but three ponies is another. We should follow this path, which is going west. It's heading for the moors, which is good, but not so useful for getting to Uncle David's. When we reach the moors we'll need to take a turn southward sooner or later.*

We set off again, and met no one. It was a sunny day, but the bridleway was dark and cool. Little golden pools of light splashed down on the brown earth, floated over the passing ponies' backs, and lit the tip of Mouse's tail. If you looked up, you saw the holes in the tree canopy above, where the gold light got in, and the leaves turned from black-green to emerald jewels so bright they hurt your eyes.

106

We walked and walked, the loose ponies stopping every so often to grab bits from the hedge, then trotting to catch us up. Once a bird took off with a clap of its wings, and they were startled and thundered up behind, shaking the ground, and I thought we'd be flattened, but the black mare stopped and bunched up her rear end like she would kick, and laid back her ears, and the other two screeched to a halt so fast they nearly sat down.

They stayed closer to us after that.

The bridleway came out of the thicket, crossed roads, and then we picked it up again in the hedge opposite. The sun traced its path in the sky to late afternoon. Hunger pointed out the time, and we stopped briefly to snack on the bits left in my bag: a wrinkly apple with crumbs on it, a crushed biscuit, a chocolate bar, and a handful of dry dog meal for Mouse. There was nothing to drink and I felt blisters burning on my feet, matching the ones on my hands.

At one point we had to go over a little bridge and right through a tiny village with just a few cottages, but we didn't see anyone except an old lady, looking out of her window and waving and smiling at the sight of the ponies, so I had to wave back.

And now, as I honestly had to admit to myself that it

wasn't late afternoon but evening, the bridleway didn't reappear, and I could see a bigger, smarter-looking village approaching.

"Oh, don't say we've got to go through there," I said. "We'll be stared at like something from the circus."

Mmm, said Mouse, sniffing around. *Path of some kind off here to the right. No sign, but it goes into woods. Let's take it.*

"I bet we're trespassing," I said, "but there isn't a gate. Perhaps the bridle path sign just fell off."

I stared into the blackness of the path, and then looked around me. A golden and red sunset had faded to lilac, shrunk down to the horizon against a sky of midnight blue. Now the last corner of light was fading over the rim of the world and taking with it all the color from the land. Everything looked like an old, faded, black-and-white photograph; the odd white flower in the hedges started to glow out strangely. The hedges seemed to send up their own mist and disappear into twilight a few meters away. Midges still danced, but their place was being taken by moths. I pushed away the thought that we might have to sleep out in the open. I had promised Tom I wouldn't. . . .

"OK, let's go."

I had all three ponies' ropes because we'd been on the road, and my arms were getting tired. I hoped I might have to lead just the black mare for a while in woods. I rubbed her forehead with the hand which held her rope and she closed her eyes appreciatively. She'd been marvelous, helping to handle the other ponies. I'd never have managed it this far without her.

We trudged along the path in what seemed at first complete blackness, but gradually my eyes became accustomed. The pale gold underside of Mouse's tail, as she carried it high and turned up at the end, seemed to attract the moonlight and picked out the way like a beacon. Somewhere above us, there was a glimpse of a bat flitting, backward, forward, hunting his path.

Suddenly, the black mare opened her eyes wide, stopped dead, and flared her nostrils, ears pricked at the track ahead. The other two ponies stopped too, and copied her.

"What is it, Mouse?"

She paused and scented the air, twitching her black nose sideways and narrowing her eyes.

Oh! With the smell of this lot in my nose, I didn't notice. Another pony ahead—not moving—and . . . a human, male human, youngish . . .

"Not moving?"

I caught up the younger mares' ropes as they were starting to look uneasy.

They are here, she said, moving round and pointing her nose slightly off the path to the right. *I think they're watching us.*

The two younger ponies started to jostle me impatiently. The black mare, head up high and everything to attention, lifted her top lip and gave a low little whinny.

They're moving, said Mouse. *They're coming toward us.*

I shortened the gray mare's rope; she was starting to get overexcited. I couldn't imagine who the watcher and his horse were, but I would be ready with a story. I wanted to look businesslike, in control, not tangled and trampled.

Peering into the darkness, I heard the slow thud of heavy hooves, saw strange, glowing, ghostly white shapes which made no sense, floating between the trees on the right. I swear I almost stopped breathing. But the ponies didn't back away in fear, they began to strain toward it, and at last, a large brown and white horse appeared, with great feathers on his lower legs; I realized the ghostly shapes had been the white patches and markings, which in the darkness had seemed to float alone. His fringe swept down long across the blaze on the center of his bowed nose, and a brown and white mane hung in waterfalls over his thick, arched neck. He snorted a welcome to the ponies. Now I could see, sitting astride his back, wide as a

110

table, there was a boy, a little older than I, and so like Tom that I caught my breath.

For a moment, I was speechless.

He stared at me, apparently as surprised as I was.

Then his eyes hardened as he took in the ponies around me.

"Who are you?" he demanded. "And what are you doing with our ponies?"

NINE
Mistaken Identity

"*Your* ponies?"

With all the shock and so on, it came out of me like a puppy yelping.

The boy didn't answer right away. He, too, seemed to be puzzled, scrunching up his brow and staring at me and then the ponies. It was as if he'd been ready and expecting something, but I wasn't it.

Mouse wagged her tail gently and looked from the boy to me and back again.

He seems all right, she said. *He's not lying, at any rate.*

I didn't know what to say and the silence was stretching like a thin elastic band. Here I was, with three ponies, which, I couldn't deny, were not mine, and maybe could even be described as stolen, but I seemed to be being accused by the wrong person.

The boy pointed to the black mare.

"That's Mary"—he moved his finger in the direction of the other ponies—"she's Bonnie, and that's Bella. They were taken from us a while ago."

He spoke patiently and less accusingly now. His horse shifted from one foot to another and blew softly at the mares.

Suddenly, as I looked up at him, I forgot all the worry and just felt grateful. He wasn't Tom, but I wished he was—anyone to take a bit of the burden.

"Are they really yours?" I said. "It would be so good if they were. I've walked for miles and my arms are hurting and I'm very tired. I thought I had to take them all the way to the moors."

All the strength seemed to leave me and I fought to keep a wobble out of my voice.

The boy looked at me oddly.

"Do you mean you *found* them? They were *straying?*" The note of suspicion had crept back.

"No, not exactly. It's a long story. They were in a paddock back on the outskirts of Tawntown—"

The boy sucked in his breath with a little "ah" sound.

"—and they were going to be killed and the man said he'd got them wild off the moor. So I just had to take them. I was trying to get them back to the moor. . . ."

I tailed off. It sounded far-fetched even to me.

"They're not from the moor—though they're that type, all right—they are ours, and they were stolen from their

113

tethers one night, when we were near Tawntown. In any case, this man couldn't have got them wild off the moor. All the wild ponies really have owners, they just live wild until the drifts every year."

He didn't sound cross with me.

"You shouldn't be out like this, not here. It's dangerous. Here, chuck me two of the ropes, the youngsters will do. I'll lead them. Can you ride?"

"Not properly. I've only ridden bareback, with a halter. . . ."

He gave me another puzzled look.

"Then why were you walking?"

"The man said they were wild," I explained, "though I *have* got on unbroken ponies. . . ."

He rolled his eyes upward.

"You wouldn't get a halter on a wild pony as easy as you did these, I can tell you."

I led the bay and gray ponies forward and passed the ropes to him.

"I thought it was a bit strange," I admitted, "how friendly they were, I mean. I wondered if he was lying."

"You get on Mary, she's quiet as a lamb. Can you do that?"

"Yep," I said, not wanting to admit that Tom usually

114

gave me a leg up. I led the black mare over to a tree stump, and using that and a handful of the long mane, managed to clamber onto her broad, black back.

"Follow me, and we'll go and sort this all out," said the boy, and I was happy for someone to take charge.

He swung his horse around in the direction he'd come from, and kept the two ponies on either side of him. Mary needed no telling, and set off automatically after them.

Mouse pushed past us: *Excuse me,* she said sniffily. *For obvious reasons of safety and hygiene, I don't particularly like following the back end of ponies. I will go up front and warn you if there's any problem.*

Where the trees narrowed, the ponies being led sort of jiggled themselves into single file and got through; I clutched the rope to the halter in my hand and swayed gently on Mary's steady back, pulling my knees in from the branches. I could just make out the luminous patch of white which circled the brown and white horse's tail in front of us.

Then the path widened again, and I thought I could hear voices ahead, and now there were lights, softly glowing.

Mouse appeared suddenly alongside me.

Be careful, she said, darting her eyes about so that I

115

could make out the whites in the dark. *Some kind of trouble. Angry people. I don't like it. Warn the boy.*

Any thought I might have had that he was leading me into a deliberate trap left my head with her last words.

I was about to call him, then realized I didn't know his name.

"Oi!" I half shouted, half whispered. "Stop a minute!" and I added a low whistle.

He heard that and pulled up. I could make him out peering back at me through the gloom.

"What is it?"

"Trouble ahead. Shhh."

I saw him turn around to face ahead, craning his neck and leaning about for a better view, like a kestrel trying to focus.

He gave out a low groan.

"Oh, hell. Well, there's nothing I can do. I'll just ride on through 'em, I suppose. You—uh, you'd better get off Mary or they'll take you for one of us. Pass me the rope."

I didn't know what he was talking about, but I did as he said.

"Wait till they've gone, or sneak through or something. Don't run away, now, will you?" He eyed me sharply. "I told you it was dangerous here at night. You come and tell my dad your story and I think he'll be pleased, all right. Promise?"

"Promise," I said, still wondering at how much he looked like Tom, then added: "What do you mean, they'll take me for one of you?"

But he had kicked the big horse into a fast trot and, with the excited ponies surging alongside him, he headed toward the voices and the lights.

I stepped out cautiously from the trees and walked slowly after him, Mouse beside me.

Moonlight lit a fenced clearing at the edge of woodland; beyond was grazing and then more woodland. A rough, wide, railed track ran up to the clearing from our right, and off, I supposed, to the road.

The lights were coming from a long, white camper parked near some kind of truck in the rough little field, and from flashlights waving in what seemed to be a crowd of people standing arguing, by the sounds of it, at the head of the track, the entrance to the clearing.

As we approached, we saw the boy steady his trot and shout at the crowd to clear the way; they seemed to look around at his call, then bunched together. He would surely trample them if they did not move. Now the horse was making a way through, and the ponies, less polite, were causing people to skip out of the way.

He was almost through; then a roar from the head of the crowd, and like an angry animal, it seemed the dark figures, flickering with light, regrouped, swamped around him, pulled at him like a wave. I saw a hand on his leg; he tipped sideways for a moment.

"No!" I shouted, and ran forward.

Mouse pressed alongside me.

Steady, now, you will get us into danger, she panted.

I pushed through the crowd, rough jackets, expensive soft coats, sharp voices of women vying with the grumbling curses of men. What was the matter with them?

"Get off him, leave him alone!" I shouted, and, pushing past the terrified gray pony, rearing and plunging at the end of her rope, I saw at last the brown and white horse's flank. I leaned up and managed to wrench a hand from the boy's ankle. There was a ripple of confusion; the crowd stopped, turned, took in its breath for a moment like a wave retreating from the shore. In that moment, the horse plunged forward, and boy and ponies were propelled toward the camper.

I had no time to see more. From somewhere, a hand

118

grabbed my arm and pulled it back behind me. Leering faces; a cropped-headed teenager, an aging, fattish man in a flat cap with red thread veins mapping his nose and cheeks, an orange-faced woman with too much lipstick; all of them sharing a light in the eye, features twisted with hate.

"Got one! He was with him! Scum! Clear out of it, all of you!"

Hands seemed to grab from everywhere, a baying went up like hounds at a kill, spittle whistled past my ear. A sharp pain in my shin and I realized I'd been kicked. My toes were trodden on.

But suddenly there was a wolf for the hounds to battle with. A deep, terrible, snarling bark, which would have done credit to Barney, ripped through the air. For a moment, I was more terrified than ever, thinking I was now being attacked by someone's dog. Then I felt the hands pull away as if by magic, and saw in front of me a huge whirling fireball of ginger and sable fury, facing the crowd which surrounded me. I almost didn't recognize Mouse. With her hair on end, she seemed to have the shoulders and build of a hyena.

"Call your dog off, or I'll sort it!" shouted a posh-sounding man near my ear.

"Call these nutters off, or I'll let *her* sort it!" I screamed back at him.

Something seemed to click. The voice shouted, "OK, folks, back off now, back off. Let him go, everyone calm down."

Voices started to echo him, like sheep. Mouse laid down her hair and shook her ears with a flapping sound but stood unmoving in front of me. Someone shone a flashlight in my face.

"Who are you?" came the posh voice. "You live here? Are you with them?"

"No, I don't. With who? I don't know what you mean."

The flashlight swung away.

"Our mistake, sorry," said the voice easily, as if nothing had happened, then to the crowd, "It's just a boy, everyone," and there were murmurs, people looked away, back toward the camper, lost interest. Someone lightly brushed down the back of my jacket. I turned to see if I could spot the owner of the voice. There he was, about a meter behind me; slick coat, smart scarf. I had been frightened, but now I was angry.

"What the hell was all that about?" I demanded.

"Sorry, and all that. Just a case of mistaken identity."

Who could they have mistaken me for, I wondered, at

my age and size, to attack me so viciously? What awful thing could this person have done?

The orange-faced woman appeared next to me. Mouse gave a low growl as she stepped too close.

"We thought you were a *Gypsy*, just for a moment, no offense meant, of course; you were close behind one so we mistook you. We are trying to move them on. I suppose you're here with someone with the same idea?" she said brightly, baring her teeth.

"No, no, I'm not. I was passing and wondered what the noise and lights were. I'm—I'm on holiday with my uncle," I said, disbelief swamping my anger so that my voice dropped to a more normal level.

"Just our local protest," she continued. "I hope no one bumped you or anything?"

I shook my head and walked back to the trees with Mouse.

Never make me do that again, said Mouse. *I nearly bit someone. Whatever was wrong with them?*

They were sorry they nearly hurt me. They think they are proper, civilized people. I think they only hurt kids who are Gypsy kids. That, of course, is different, I explained, still fuming. *I have to get to the camper and keep my word, Mouse. Besides, we have nowhere else to stay.*

Hold up a bit. In the trees and behind the camper, quick. Looks like police are coming, said Mouse, steering me by pushing my leg and almost tripping me up.

We circled and managed to end up behind the camper. A blue light pulsed against the tree trunks, lit up the tussocks of grass. Raised voices rang out again. I saw dark uniformed figures spreading out, while others directed the crowd, pointing away down the track toward the road. Angry fingers wagged almost in their faces. I couldn't see their expressions beneath their helmets and caps.

They're checking for more troublemakers, said Mouse. *They'll ask us what we're doing here in a minute.*

I suddenly realized the danger we were in—my journey could be over now, both of us shipped back up north and home, Mouse's fate the same as the day I'd set out.

"Under the camper, quick!" I said to Mouse, pulling my bag from my back, and I was down and crawling, belly in the grass, wriggling beneath the metal. Mouse shimmied under next to me, scraping her back on the edge of the camper. As footsteps grew closer, I inched my bag after us, just in the nick of time. Black boots came into our tiny view, tramped past, paused, clumped away again. We heard a muffled curse as the owner met a bramble.

122

We waited for what seemed like ages. Mouse crawled away to look out at the front.

The mad people are all going—they've gone, she reported. We heard the camper door opening, low voices of men; "We'll wish you a quiet night, then, sir, we'll sit out on the road awhile longer to make sure . . ." The tramp of boots again, the police car starting up, driving away.

And I lay and thought and thought. The boy on the brown and white horse was a Gypsy. Of course. Smacked you in the face, when you thought about it. The ponies had been taken from their tethers. While they were near Tawntown. Why had I been so slow? I remembered the Gypsy family who'd stayed near our village. The little girl who'd come to school for a while, with shining hair and spotless, old-fashioned clothes. She was clever, like me and Tom, and got bored by the too-easy lessons. She had it worse than us, because for some reason the teacher gave her even easier work and seemed to think she was stupid. My mum going all still one day when I got home from school and told her I didn't think Phoebe was going to come to school again; she'd had enough, one of the boys had called her a dirty Gypsy, which was stupid, wasn't it, as she had to be the cleanest kid in the whole school?

"She's the cleanest kid in the whole school because her

mother washes her clothes by hand every day," said my mum. "I've seen her myself."

"I think kids can be too clean," I said. "I don't think her mum needs to make such a fuss."

"Oh yes she does," said my mum, and I wondered why her voice was wobbling. "More than any ordinary person. Because of people like that boy who called her names."

She slapped down the washing basket and looked out of the window. I could tell she was angry, but I couldn't think what I had said or done. I stayed quiet and still. At that moment, past the window of the kitchen, a woman walked with a baby in her arms. It was Phoebe's mum. My mother snatched up a box of eggs she'd collected that day from the chickens, and now I was astonished to see she had tears welling in her eyes as she strode out of the door and down the path.

I peeked out of the window and saw her thrust them at Phoebe's mum wordlessly; then she stalked back up the path to the house again. Phoebe's mum stood puzzled for a moment, raised her hand gently in thanks toward me. I waved back and she carried on her way. Mum hadn't talked to me about her odd behavior that day, and Phoebe never came back to school. Now I was starting to understand.

124

It's quiet, now, said Mouse. *Shall we get out from here, whenever you're ready?*

"Sorry, Mouse, I was just thinking."

I pulled myself forward to be alongside her, so that we would come out by the front door and steps; but just as I wriggled clear, a great pair of hands clamped on my shoulders from above and a voice cried:

"Gotcha!"

TEN
On the Road at Night

I was jerked up off my feet by the most powerful grip I'd ever felt. The hands on my shoulders were massive, like grizzly bear paws. I yelped, and Mouse was out from under the camper in a jiffy, cursing and barking, but there wasn't much she could do. In a flash, I was being hauled backward through the doorway and inside the camper.

I saw the door kicked shut in front of me, a second before Mouse must have thudded into it. I heard her barking and scrabbling at it, but I still hadn't got a look at whoever had grabbed me.

I kicked and struggled for all I was worth, but felt my arms trapped by my sides, and a gruff man's voice called out, "Whoa, steady there, hold still!"

Partly because of that, but mainly because I couldn't do much else, I stopped fighting. I blinked. It was warm and fuzzy with soft light inside the camper. I was aware of being stared at by a whole crowd of people.

A voice came from behind my head—the owner of the voice being the person who'd got ahold of me, I supposed.

"Caught him under the vardo. I told you they hadn't all gone. About to set a fire, I'll bet!"

"No I wasn't!" I shouted. "What sort of idiot would do that?"

It had gone very still. Even Mouse had stopped barking. I looked around slowly and took in an old man, dressed in farming-type clothes, white shirt, neckerchief, waistcoat; a youngish woman in the shadows behind him, clutching a baby; the tops of some tiny kids' heads peeking out from behind her so you could just see their eyes; and over to the other side of me, a little, old, square-shaped woman with a fuzz of gray hair. Every one of them was staring at me, openmouthed.

"*What?*" I said.

There was a sound of a sort of gasp turning into a chuckle, starting from the old man and spreading among them.

He moved forward into the light to look at me more closely. His face was lined and weathered like an old shoe; his eyes, crinkled deep and serious, studied mine.

"Now, now, then, let's all calm down a little. Bill, leave go of his arms, let's see what we have here."

The bear paws reluctantly loosened, though I felt that Bill waited ready to pounce again if necessary. I shrugged

127

my jacket straight irritably, and stuck my chin up, trying to drag back a bit of dignity. Bill's voice rumbled from behind me.

"It's a flipping Gorgio, in any case. . . ."

"I don't know," said the old man, his eyes taking in every detail of my appearance. I started to feel like an object. Why the heck didn't they just ask me who I was?

"I don't know what you're talking about," I said. "I'm not a Gypsy, I'm not a flipping Gorgio, whatever that is, and I'm not an 'it.'"

At that moment the door of the camper opened, and the boy from the brown and white horse entered and stopped and stared at me in surprise. "I'm just a *boy*!" I shouted, and waved my arm in his direction. "Like *him*!"

Mouse shot through the door, pushed past the boy's legs, and pressed herself against my shins.

Now what? she said. *Are you all right?*

"Dad!" said the boy. "Leave him be! I told him to come and see you. I found him when I was checking the little path behind us for strangers. He brought the ponies back. I've just tethered them up."

There were cries of surprise and joy from the group now, and they pushed toward the door of the camper to look out. The boy opened the door wide and pointed, the children clamoring for a view.

"That's it, look, they're all there—Mary, Bonnie, and Bella, safe and sound," he said. Even Bill moved from behind me and peered above the heads. He wasn't as tall as I'd thought, but pretty heavily built, with legs set wide to carry it.

Then the older lady told everyone to shut the door and keep the cold out, and they all turned and looked at me again, and there was an awkward sort of pause, which she filled by saying, "Now, we are sorry, but we are likely to be jumpy with people acting wild. Who's to know if they might burn down the vardo—or camper, you'd call it. But what a way to treat a guest, who brought back what was taken from us." She twinkled light gray eyes at me, then turned to the big man and said, "Come on, Bill, give the boy a sit-down and Tom can explain and we can all have a warm drink."

"Tom?" I asked, looking around in disbelief at the boy who looked so like my brother. He smiled and nodded. "That's me."

"Did you think he was called something else, now?" asked the old lady, noticing my surprise and pausing as she put something on the little stove.

"No, it's just—my brother is Tom and he looks just like him," I blurted out. Was I giving out more information than I should? What was my story going to be this time?

Bill coaxed me to a long sort of sofa, dark red plush peeking from beneath tight plastic covers. It ran along two sides of what looked like a sitting and dining room in one, which took up about half of the camper.

I sat down and it felt fine. The place was prettied up with lots of shiny things, silver plates and china horses and pictures with big gold frames. The light danced over it all, hissing from real old-fashioned gas lamps dotted about. More warm yellow light and a wall of heat pulsed from a gas fire in front of me. I didn't realize how long it had been since I'd been comfortable. My toes started to throb where they'd been trodden on and the graze on my shin began to sing out about the state it was in.

Mouse curled up on my feet, still looking wary. You could never tell with people, after all. Everyone had been acting pretty strange today.

"Thank you," said Tom, sitting next to me, "for getting that fool off my leg. I really thought I would stick on, but I was losing my grip, what with Charlie and the three ponies to deal with."

"Charlie—is he the brown and white horse?" I asked.

He nodded, but Bill, who'd sat down opposite, asked, "Did they try to have a go at you, then, Tom? If I'd seen that, I'd have been out there. . . ."

"Better you weren't," said the old man, "and sounds like this lad dealt with it all right. Now then, let's hear about these ponies."

So, with a steaming mug of tea in my hand, I told them about where I'd found the ponies and how I'd had to save them.

They nodded from time to time, as if the strange story made sense, and despite the way they'd first treated me seemed to believe me straightaway, as Tom had when I'd met him.

The younger woman, who I'd now worked out must be Tom's mum and Bill's wife—judging from the fuss she made of Tom—hadn't said much, but now she looked at me closely, rather like the old man had earlier.

"So if you weren't with that crowd out there, and you walked all the way from Tawntown, where are your parents? Aren't they worried about you?"

There was a bit of a pause. The old man looked at me in a way which seemed to say he knew the whole truth already, which he couldn't possibly, but he was going to sit back and enjoy watching me come up with something. This was very off-putting.

I've told you I'm pretty straight-talking in general, with the odd white lie here and there, just to give people what they want. But I hadn't figured on lying to people who for once believed me and were sitting here, trusting what I was saying. So I tried to get away with just leaving bits out.

I took a deep breath.

"I am supposed to be getting to my uncle David's, on holiday for a bit while my mum copes with my brother, who's really sick. I got off the train too early and I've tried to walk or taken a lift the rest of the way."

"With yer dog here," put in the old man.

"Er, yes, with the dog." It did seem a bit odd, now he pointed it out. I added, hoping the explanation would do: "She goes everywhere with me."

"Mmm, I can see that," he said, rubbing his chin and looking thoughtfully at Mouse. She was tidying her toenails. "Dog's feet are sore. She's not been used to roads, I reckon. You've darned near walked the legs off her." He looked at me closely again.

"Trekking about with a dog on no leash, riding ponies,

but only bareback—you sure you're not a Gypsy, now, boy?" And he laughed, and so did the others, but only kindly.

"Well, I don't reckon so," I said. "I don't mind if I am. But I'd rather be just a boy. It seems a bit complicated, being a Gypsy, or being one of those—what did you call them?"

"Gorgios," said Tom. "It just means, not a Gypsy."

"Gorgios, then. If that's the mad lot who were out tonight, I don't want to be one of those, either. I think I'll stick with being me."

This seemed to go down well; they laughed and shook their heads and looked sort of sad at the same time. But Bill, Tom's dad, added, quite casually, "And who is 'me' then? You haven't even given us your name, lad."

There wasn't any point in lying. I hoped I wasn't plastered over every headline in the country, but I guessed that was sort of unlikely, being just one kid and a dog missing from a tiny village no one ever heard of, way up north.

"John," I said, "John Hawkins. And this is Mouse."

"Pleased to meet you," said Bill, and he and the old man reached forward and we shook hands properly in turn, which was hard, considering the hot mug of tea.

133

"Well," said Bill's mum, like any good mother, not letting go of her first question, "that's all very well. But you won't have arrived at your uncle's, so surely your mum must be worried, or he must be, by now? Didn't we ought to let them know you're safe?"

Bill said, "Now, she's right, of course. If you're missing, and someone finds out you're with us, why, the Gypsies will have stolen a child. We're supposed to have done that, you know, in the old days, though why the heck we should want to, with this lot crowding out the vardo, I don't know."

The two littler kids, who seemed shy, giggled at this and clutched at their mother. They looked like Tom, with their floppy dark hair and doe eyes.

I still didn't say anything for a moment; Mouse stayed quiet at my feet. I cast a look toward the old man. For some reason, I felt he knew.

"It's true enough, young man," he said, "for all he jokes. We wouldn't want to be accused of kidnapping, now. Or aiding a runaway." He saw, I swear, the jolt that went through me at that word, though I moved not a muscle.

"Do you have an address for this uncle who expects you?"

"Yes, yes, I do," I said quickly. "He lives at Easteep, his name is David Hawkins. His address is here, in my bag."

134

Don't let him ask if I have the phone number, I thought, please don't phone him. He might still say he doesn't expect or want me and to get my mother to fetch me back. . . .

"Well, then, that's all right, I reckon. We are already packed up this evening and heading to a site right by there. Isn't that lucky? We'll take you right to him. Seems the quickest and easiest? Is that all right?"

"Yes, yes," I faltered. It was perfect. But now the time was upon me, I worried about Uncle David's reaction. It was the summit of our plan, but it was the bit we were least sure about. I pushed the doubt out of my head. I had come all this way to do my best and the end was nearly in sight. I was tired and bruised and hungry and thirsty and I didn't want a night out in the cold, miles from my goal. Suddenly, I was really grateful, and added, "That would be just fine, if you're sure it's all right." And everyone heard the truth in my words, and seemed to relax. They knew this part of the story, at least, was true.

I could have dropped off to sleep right there, it was so cozy; but now everyone got up and started busying themselves, packing up and so forth. It was amazing how everything got folded, stacked, and disappeared into little cubbyholes all over the place. The sofa I was sitting on lifted up like a lid and there was space to stash the children's toys and all kinds of things inside it. Everyone, even the little kids, seemed to have a job to do, and knew it well, so that I felt kind of in the way and a bit useless.

"Can I help?" I asked Tom's mum.

"Give Tom a hand loading the ponies, if you like." She smiled, and I followed him out of the warm camper into the dark night; Mouse following, yawning and stretching.

No hope of dinner, I suppose, she said, *and me with the legs nearly walked off my body.*

"Mouse, I am sorry," I said, "I completely forgot. I haven't got any food left. Do your paws hurt a lot?"

Tom turned around, surprised. I had spoken out loud.

"The way she's limping, I'd reckon they do," he said. "Even if she can't answer you. Give her some grub first, then give me a hand. You can put salt water on the paws, but if she's no more walking to do, I'd leave them alone and they'll be all right. While you're talking to her, tell her not to chew them too much. Some dogs worry at them and make them worse." And he walked away again toward the tethered ponies, and I didn't know how much he was joking.

Oops, said Mouse, grinning up at me. *Don't forget, people who talk to themselves, or even to dogs, are nuts. Get on*

136

with the food, like he said. Forget the salt water, if you don't mind, and I will attempt to restrain myself from chewing off my own feet.

I doubled back to the camper, and when the old lady saw me she told me to wait, then gave me a bowl with meat scraps, sour milk, and some stale bread. "I would just have thrown it out," she explained.

It made a massive pile. I put the bowl down uncertainly in front of Mouse. *I'm not sure you'll like . . .* I began—silently, this time.

Ah! Heaven and bliss and only what I deserve, said Mouse, tucking in. *Now leave me alone and do those ponies.*

I did as she said, and was in time to lead Bella, the gray mare, up the ramp of the horse trailer. Tom had put Mary in first, because she was sensible and it encouraged the others to follow her in. It was exciting, hearing the drumming of hooves next to me, as I ran firmly up the ramp like Tom had told me, in case Bella lost courage halfway up and tried to back off or turn around. Inside the trailer, the air was warm and steamy with the smell of horse. Tom jumped up next to me to tie up Bella's rope. I gave Mary's dark nose a rub, then got out of the way as Tom hurried Bonnie, the bay, up the ramp.

The ponies were turned to stand sideways, and finally

137

Charlie was brought in, more slowly, his huge hooves clumping up the ramp calmly. Once tied sideways, he completely hid the little ponies behind him.

"Tom," I said, as we lifted the ramp to close the box, "isn't it late to be setting off? You're not all heading off quick because of me, are you?"

Tom pushed the bolt home on his side to secure the ramp and I did the same.

"Of course not. It's quieter traveling at night. Besides, Granddad's getting twitchy about the sort of people you met tonight. My mum is more and more worried because of the kiddies, the babe and all that. They want us off and out of here. Seems easier if we go."

We were walking back to the camper.

"Why did they want you out? Do they own this land?"

"No, it's ours. Granddad's bought it fair and square. But it seems it makes no difference. We only stopped here because all the other sites were full. Now there's room for us for a while on the site down near your uncle, we'll be better off there. No water or electricity here, in any case. That's why we've had to drag out the old gas lamps."

Back to the camper, and the gas cylinders had been hauled inside and everyone seemed to be waiting for us.

Bill and Tom's mum and one of the kiddies were going

in the cab of the trailer, and everyone else was cramming into the big old transit van which was already hitched up to the camper. Mouse happily agreed to bed down in the camper, and so one small dog had more room than any of us. Someone said, "*Si tut bocklo?* Are you hungry?" and pushed a pasty into my hand. I squashed in next to Tom, a stack of garden furniture, and tools. Somewhere in the dark a chicken clucked, rustled, and settled. The old man started up the engine, and the headlights came on and lit the trees and the head of the track. Then we were off. The baby, buckled into a seat next to me, began snoozing almost straightaway, to my relief. I watched as its eyelids grew heavier and its lashes lowered to its cheeks.

I wanted to talk some more to Tom, but before I knew what was happening, I must have fallen asleep too.

Then I was dreaming, and I wasn't sure if it was my brother Tom's dream or mine, but my dad was there, smiling, and he'd just been working—away, far away, in China maybe, he said—and he was going back again, and taking Tom with him, and Mouse, but not me; for some reason, I had to stay. I would be all alone, and though everyone seemed to think it was normal, and sensible, I knew, I just knew, that I'd never see any of them again, and I was trying to shout "No!" and "Stop!" but he was turning away

139

and taking Tom's hand and Mouse was already trotting away ahead of them, toward the mountain behind our cottage; and the sound just wouldn't come out of my mouth, and I couldn't move my legs and there was nothing, nothing I could do.

ELEVEN
Finding What You Look For

Tom gave me a nudge. I found I'd nodded off on his shoulder, which was a bit embarrassing, but at least I didn't seem to have dribbled.

"Bad dream?" Tom asked.

I wasn't quite awake. *I hope it was a dream*, I thought, but just said, "Whassup? Why have we stopped?" and rubbed my eyes.

"We're here, you fool."

Feet tramped around outside, and there was a scraping of metal which hurt the underneath of my nails to hear it, and then the doors were pulled open.

"Already?" I asked, waiting my turn to clamber out.

"It wasn't far. You're too used to walking," said Tom, giving me a hand to jump down.

The cold night air was sweet, fanning my face with a tang of crushed grass and hedgerow. The back of the van had smelled, not surprisingly, of garden furniture, tools, chickens, and baby.

My feet were on concrete. I looked around me, and we

seemed to be in a large yard, with walls. There were other campers, lights glowing, curtains twitching. I saw that our camper was already slotted in, unhitched. Someone had opened the door for Mouse, and she was mooching about as if she'd lived here all her life. When she saw me, her ears went up and her tail wagged and she galloped over like a puppy.

Nearly there, she said. *I can smell salt, water, and fish—it must be the water you talked about, the sea!*

Bill was backing the trailer into another space.

The old man took Tom and me to one side. He fixed me with a firm look.

"Now, John Hawkins, have you ever stayed with this uncle before?"

"No," I answered.

"Get the address out and read it to me, can you? We want you there tonight, late as it might be."

I pulled out the crumpled paper from my bag, and managed to read it by the inside light of the van, which flared out from the open back doors.

"Goldtor, Easteep, it says. Not a house number or road, though . . ."

"Tiny place, only one or two houses, that's why. I know it right enough. Beautiful spot. No more than ten minutes by pony. Tom, take Charlie and Mary to be safer and quicker. See him right in the house, then I want you back here. All right?"

Tom nodded.

I held out my hand. The old man reached out and shook it.

"Thank you, thank you very much. I am sorry to put you to trouble."

"Thank *you*, John. No trouble. A return of a favor for getting the ponies and helping Tom get through the mob. *Kushti bok*."

I tried to say it back to him.

Tom helped out.

"*Kushti bok*," he said carefully, and I managed to repeat it to his granddad, and we all smiled. "It means good luck," he explained, and I went round shaking hands and saying it to all the family.

Bill had Charlie and the other ponies out now, ready to put in the paddock nearby. I rubbed Bonnie and Bella's faces and hugged their necks goodbye. I watched Tom place his hands up high on Charlie's back and simply spring from a standstill, landing perfectly astride. Bill saw my expression and laughed.

"Just takes practice," he said. "Don't worry, I'll give you

a leg up." And he held Mary's rope in one hand and made a step with his hand for my knee, lifting me so powerfully that when I was in midair, I almost flew over the other side.

"Country roads, it's dark, and you've no lights," he said sternly to Tom. "Won't be much traffic, maybe none, but when there is, it's maybe a young hotshot going too fast. Stick on the side, all right?"

"All right, Dad, I'll be back quick. Come on, John. I know where it is." And Tom wheeled Charlie round and jog-trotted toward the road, sparks showering from his hooves in the darkness. I gripped tight with my legs as Mary spun and followed, out into the dark night, Mouse darting along in front of us joyfully, her sore paws forgotten, with the calls of Bonnie and Bella ringing behind us.

No traffic passed us, just the flitter of something in the corner of my eye every now and again, which was all I could catch of a little bat in the moonlight, out hunting moths back and forth, back and forth. The ponies' hooves made a soft thudding sound on the grass of the shoulder alongside the hedgerow. When the shoulder became too steep or disappeared, we made a ringing clatter, but no one seemed to be around to hear it.

Almost there, almost there, Mouse said from time to time, sometimes rushing on ahead, sometimes stopping to sniff something exciting.

High up in the dark, we heard faint birdcalls, and tilting our heads, we saw a few gulls beating their steady way south; then Tom turned Charlie up a narrow ribbon of road which dropped away below us and up again, and pointed. Between the rising hills which I now realized were cliffs, a clear, calm space glittered whitely. "The sea!" I whispered.

Just look at all that swimming, said Mouse. *It's the biggest swimming thing I ever saw. I can't wait.*

Tom pointed to the hill which towered over the ocean. Green and gold at the top, even in the darkness, giving way either side to dark pines.

"Goldtor," he called back, stopping Charlie and leaning a hand on his rump. "See the top? Bracken and yellow gorse flowers."

There didn't seem to be a house on it.

"He lives up there?" I asked doubtfully.

"No, there's nothing living there but rabbits," Tom laughed. "Your uncle's house is just named after it. Here's Easteep."

And I looked along the road and made out one or two gateways cut from the hedge, and trees through which you could see the odd stone wall of a cottage.

I rode Mary up alongside him.

Why are we stopping? asked Mouse. *Is this it?*

"Do you know which house it is?" I asked Tom. My heart was thumping hard up high in my chest. It was almost in my throat. It sounded out through my words.

"I do," said Tom, "we've been coming round here for years, our family, for generations. Not this cottage, but the next one." He looked across at me. "What's this Uncle David like?"

"I, um, I don't really know," I said. "I heard he doesn't talk much, that's all. I hope . . . I hope. . . ."

Tom kept up a steady gaze.

"He doesn't know you're coming, does he?"

"Well, no," I admitted. I didn't see the point in lying now, and it was just too hard to do with this boy.

"You run away from your dad? Your mum?"

"No, well, not on purpose. I just needed to get Mouse here safe. Mum was going to get rid of her. My brother— you know, I told you he was sick—he was all upset. He didn't think he'd get better if Mouse was put to sleep.

They wouldn't listen. They said she might bring infection. They were going to send her to the pound."

"I might have guessed," said Tom, not looking very surprised or cross. "Do you spend your whole time running around the country saving animals? Let's hope Uncle David likes dogs, let alone his nephew, then."

I looked down at Mary's dark mane, rippling away in the darkness. He was right, of course. It was one thing for an uncle to be polite to a nephew, on a visit, even if it wasn't planned. But late at night, with a dog, and asking—asking what? That he keep the dog for a year, and then return it? To people miles and miles away, that he'd hardly met?

"John," came Tom's voice, "we're here now, anyway. I'm to wait and see he takes you in. If not, you'll come back and be safe with us, but we'll have to tell someone and they'll have to get you home."

I nodded. And then it would all be for nothing, this huge journey, and I would look the biggest fool in the world.

"But the dog—if it matters that much, and he won't take her—she's fine with us, too. OK?"

I looked across at him. My heart leaped, bounced around in my chest.

"Just for a year? And we could have her back? You mean it?"

"Of course. You'd have to have her back. We just lost our dog, but Granddad isn't looking to replace her. He's going to sell the plot of land and buy a house. Bricks and mortar. We won't travel anymore."

"Oh, thank you, Tom, thank you. I mean, I hope it won't be needed. We'd pay for the dog food and everything. But—why are you not going to travel anymore? Why don't you keep the land?"

It was Tom's turn to look down at his horse's mane.

"It's too hard, nowadays. There aren't enough sites and there's nowhere for us to stop. Then, like you saw tonight, settled people ignore or attack you. My mum's had enough. She wants the children safe, and she wants them to live in a house like everyone else and go to school and we won't tell anyone we're Gypsies, and you get treated just fine."

"That doesn't seem right," I said.

"No, but it's easier," said Tom, nudging Charlie with his legs to walk on.

"I suppose so," I said, uneasily. We passed a drive, then halted at the next.

Mouse looked at me.

You know what he's talking about, she said. *Hiding what you are. You, of all people, can't argue with it. This house, is it?*

"Go on," said Tom. "I'll watch from the end of the drive. Jump off now and chuck me Mary's rope."

I looked up the drive and saw the house was in view. It was low and of old stone, but larger than a cottage. The garden looked wild and rambling.

"Lights are on," said Tom. "At least you won't be waking him up."

I slipped off Mary and hugged her neck goodbye.

Mouse waited impatiently.

Before I could take a step toward the house, lights flooded the path from the other side of the hedge and a neighbor's voice called out angrily: "Who's there? Is that Gypsies? What are you up to?"

"Nothing, sir," called out Tom shakily. "Visiting."

The front door of Uncle David's house opened. I couldn't make out the figure very well in the darkness.

He seemed to look in our direction and called to his neighbor over the hedge as he walked toward us: "Kindly mind your own business, Joe Blunt, as I mind mine."

And then he was right up close, but he didn't notice me, standing in the dark next to the black mare, just said to Tom, "All right, son? The roadside is free for any man to graze his horse on."

And for a moment he looked like he was going to turn back to the house, but then Mouse trotted up and stood in front of him.

I heard her say, *It's me and John; we've come to stay. Is that all right?* and he stopped and stared as if he was turned to stone for a moment in the moonlight.

Then he looked away from her and all around and saw me.

"John? Is that—*John?*"

And I saw his face as the moon passed from behind a cloud, and I saw the turn of his head, the pattern of his hair, the way he stood, and the note in his voice, and it was my dad, my precious dad, and I just said, "Da. Da. Da . . ." and couldn't finish the word, because it couldn't be, and then I rushed up and grabbed him and he was real, and solid and not a ghost, and not dead, and I didn't care. I cried and cried and cried.

TWELVE
Brothers

I felt Mouse jump up and put her paws on my hip.

John! she said. *John, no.*

Then two hands, so familiar, gently took my shoulders. I felt a big hand wiping my face. I opened my eyes, sniffing up tears as hard as I could. Now he was crouched down so his face was at my level. He tipped up my chin.

"Da—" I still stammered.

His brown eyes, I thought I'd forgotten, but now I knew so well, looked back at me. Some deep sadness moved behind them.

"David," he said gently, then, more firmly, "That's right, I'm David." I stared at him and the world fell away, and I seemed to go with it, everything whirled, pieces flew, and finally came back together—differently.

He was older, a little shorter; his hair was a lighter brown and curled less; his manner was quieter, his shoes were not quite of the same type. He was very, very like— but he was not, after all, my dad.

Oh, John, I'm sorry, Mouse was saying, snuffling my

151

hands, reaching, trying to lick the salt water from my face. *I always thought you understood. But after all, you're only a puppy. This could never be Dad. Dad's gone, really gone. This is David, the brother.*

"All right, John?" said Tom, gently across the night air. Charlie shuffled, Mary snorted.

I had forgotten he was there. He had waited, as he had promised he would, to see everything was all right. He must have seen me crying.

I looked at him.

"Yes, yes, I'm sorry, Tom, to make you wait."

Uncle David said, "Do you want to come in too, have a drink?"

"No thank you," said Tom, "I'm expected. You two be all right?"

"Of course," said Uncle David.

"Then I'll be off." He leaned down from Charlie, and offered me his hand.

As I shook it, I looked at Tom and now I saw him differently. He *was* a little like my brother, but not very—stockier, darker, with as many things different as there were similar. But his eyes fastened on mine.

"Kushti bok, Pral."

"What's the last bit mean?" I sniffed.

"Brother," he said.

I smiled for what seemed like the first time in ages.

"Yeah," I said, "*pral*. We can be brothers if we want. *Kushti bok, pral.*"

Then he pulled Charlie's head away from the tasty grass, brought Mary alongside him, and headed out to the road, calling back: "We're here for a while now. Don't forget to drop by."

And the hooves rang out as they trotted off into the night.

We watched him go and then Uncle David steered me by the shoulder in the direction of the house.

"Come on, John. Sounds like we have some sorting out to do."

Mouse said, *You're telling me. And some food and drink and sleep wouldn't hurt him.*

And Uncle David said, out loud, "Don't worry, dog, I do know all that."

EPILOGUE
Sorting Out

Uncle David put on toast and fried eggs and a kettle and then sat me down in his dark, old-fashioned lounge and made me listen as he phoned my mum. After he'd broken the news to her—he pulled his ear away a bit from the receiver and I winced at the noise she was making—he passed the phone to me and went back to the kitchen.

To cut a long story short, she was, of course, cross, tearful, happy, and then cross again, and so on, for some time, as you'd expect, but it wasn't so bad, and I felt a lot better once it was over and done with. Tom hadn't been at all well, but had managed to sort of hint that I was around the neighborhood, or at least, didn't put them off the idea. They had believed I was local, hiding out somewhere, and had never dreamed I would have gone so far. She was now going to ring around to the local police and all the kind people who had helped to look for me. At that I felt even more guilty.

Then she wanted to talk to Uncle David again, so I got him back from the kitchen and passed the phone to him.

You could tell it was true, he didn't talk much, and he hated the phone. He held it like he wasn't used to it and said the least he had to, in an awkward sort of voice. I went back to the kitchen and buttered the toast and saved the eggs from going hard and poured the tea.

When he'd finished talking—or mostly listening—to Mum, he just rubbed his face with his hands and then all over his hair till it stood up a bit crazily, and looked at me and sighed.

"Why didn't I know Tom was ill? After all, he is my nephew."

"I don't suppose they thought to ring you," I said, not wanting to repeat Mum and Gran's opinion that he wouldn't be interested in having Mouse, and that he was "a very taciturn man" and "much too far away."

"No, no, you're right. I have never phoned your family. Even when your dad was brought here for the funeral, they did the phoning and arranging. It's my fault as much as anyone's. Terrible, terrible how these things happen. I'm not good with the phone and so on; my wife, when she was alive, she would have been the one. She did all the birthday and Christmas cards, kept in touch. Ah well." And he sighed, and his eyes went to a photo of a smiling, pretty woman over the fireplace, hugging a boy and a girl.

"Are those your children?" I asked.

He came to, as if he'd been miles away, and said, "Of course! Didn't you know? These are your cousins!" and seized the photo and passed it to me.

"That's Dan, named after your dad; he's all grown up now, works in London; and that's Daisy, off around the world, probably in Peru at the moment."

"I have cousins!" I said, and stared at the photo. They looked familiar, and like nice people. I thought for a moment. "Dad did say, now I think back. But it's hard to remember or understand when you're younger." Also, I realized privately, I hadn't thought about Dad or anything he'd said much, after his death. Perhaps I had put away and forgotten lots of things at that time. Locked them away with the pain of remembering him, a whole bunch of little facts and phrases, important and unimportant.

The upshot of it all was, I was to stay for a week or so, even though I would miss the start of school. "I can take time off work," Uncle David said. "They're always on at me to take a holiday. Now there's a good reason."

"What do you work as?" I asked. I couldn't imagine. He looked like a cross between a gardener and a writer or artist, maybe.

"I'm a professor," he said unexpectedly.

He didn't say anything about Mouse, who was curled up in front of the fire on an old sweater he'd put down for her. When I asked, terrified of the answer, he stopped munching his toast and looked at me as if I were mad.

"Of course she'll stay with me. For as long as you need." Then he went back to his food.

That night was for sleeping. I had Dan's old room, with a big, warm, comfortable bed, and still with his boy stuff in: a dusty telescope, a globe which wobbled like it would come off its stand if you turned it, piles of books and circuit boards where something had been taken to pieces and never put back together again. I felt like I knew him even though I hadn't met him yet.

I dreamed that night of the crowded station again, but this time, instead of my seeing it just through Tom's eyes, he was in the dream with me. I saw him searching, pale, with hunted eyes, the figure of a man seeming to follow him. I pushed my way through the people, with Mouse trotting by my side.

"Tom!" I called. "She's here! We're here!"

He looked up and saw us and relief smoothed the frown from his face; the killer from the Wanted poster was behind him, but as we drew closer to Tom, the man looked more harmless, and his features less and less like the face

157

on the poster, until he was walking away, just an ordinary passerby.

And now as we hugged, Tom and I, and Mouse leaped up between us and had to be hugged in turn, I saw the color running back to his skin, and the mischievous glint return to his eyes, and felt the power in the crushing grip of his arms.

This was a special dream, as it turned out later. I had had Tom's dreams before, and he had had mine, but *this* one . . . We talked later, and we'd had the same dream at the same time.

"I knew you were safe, home and dry," he told me then, "and the surge through my body—it was like a great, green plant sprouting somewhere in my feet and running like Jack's beanstalk all through me, till I felt strong and tall as the big oak in Mr. Jones's field. Right from that moment, I knew I was getting better."

The next day, Uncle David sat me down and made me tell him the whole story of my journey, the planning and everything. So I did, just like you've read it here. He didn't say much, just groaned at particular points, like when me and Tom decided it was the best course of action, the story of Sage's mum and poor Mr. Green, Pete's dad and his terrible research, the crowd who tried to pull Tom from Charlie.

"Right," he said, matter-of-factly, at the end. "There's nothing I can do for any of these people, but let's sort out Barney. I think I know who the man is, or at least, where he used to work."

And whatever he felt about talking and using the phone, he picked it up and told me to take Mouse down to the beach and let her have the swim she kept going on about, if I could avoid drowning, falling off the rocks, or rescuing any animals.

I promised him I could, and went off and left him to it.

When we came back, he said Barney was being picked up by the police and a charity, and they'd been warned he must be muzzled but on no account was to be destroyed. He knew the best dog shrink in the country, and this guy had promised to try and fix the damage.

Then after lunch, during which he kept sighing and looking thoughtfully at me, he suddenly announced we were going for a little ride in the car.

I waited as he got it out of the garage. It was old, but very big, shiny, and posh. Inside, the seats were real leather and the dash was walnut. "Where are we going?"

I asked. I had learned that Uncle David did talk, but you had to ask him to.

"To see your dad," he said.

And so I found myself in a windy churchyard, staring at my dad's name at the bottom of a big old stone in front of tussocky, clipped grass. The writing higher up was ancient and worn away, almost impossible to read, but David explained that this was where his and my dad's parents were buried—my grandparents, who I'd never met, as they were dead long before I was born—and that gave me a funny feeling, thinking they were only like Gran, back at home, and I might have known and liked them, if things had been different. DANIEL HAWKINS and his date of birth and death were firmly carved, and staring at that stone and the figures upon it, there was no getting away from it. Already the weather had begun to work its softening fingers over the letters and the numbers. Already moss was creeping, blurring. Years had gone by. But I was only just getting it.

Uncle David sat down and waited and soon I asked questions and he talked back; what they had done as boys, how they'd lived, how they'd grown. He'd gone into medicine, my dad had done philosophy and sociology, but of course, I'd know that.

"No," I said, "I didn't. I just knew he had 'learning.' "

160

Uncle David looked surprised.

"Didn't your mum tell you?"

"She doesn't talk about him much." Then I added, "I don't know why, she always seems—sort of—cross with him, or something."

Uncle David shook his head.

"People cope with grief and loss in lots of different ways," he said. "I remember, when my wife died, going through that cross bit. It's almost easier to be cross than sad all the time."

I thought about that. Maybe as I had coped by locking everything about Dad away behind my memory, Mum had coped by doing the same, and becoming irritable when the subject came up. Perhaps that was why she had been down on Mouse, and so quick to just push her out. Dad had brought her to us, she was another reminder of him.

Uncle David had been thinking too. He found it hard to talk in big bursts.

"But your mum loved him to bits, you know, and he loved her. Why, he even threw away everything, insisted on going back to live in her home village, because he knew she missed it and worried about her mother."

I stared at him.

"No, no, it was Mum made him live there. Then he

couldn't get work, in spite of his degrees. She didn't seem to like them because of that."

"Well, to be honest, she has a point. Daniel would have found it hard to get much work in those subjects anywhere. And she tried to be brave and live down in the city, for the sake of finding work. She tried to talk him out of moving back up north. But he knew her heart lay there. And no one was offering him much in the city in any case. So, no, it's not really any one person's fault your family ended up living where and how you do. I think," he said, "you and your mum and Tom have got a bit of talking to do. I know she had a point, keeping young children away from a funeral, but I think it might have been better if you'd come, after all. Come on, let's go back now. There is still more sorting to be done."

I didn't know what he meant, but it came clear over time. First, he was a professor, and he got hold of everyone he could who knew about Tom's illness. This involved a lot of phoning, which must have hurt, but he did it. He told me everything was being done that could be, and Tom was in good hands. There was a specialist in the city, though, who could also take a look at him.

At the end of the week, he got Dan to come down and stay for a few days to look after Mouse while he drove me all the way home. Dan was tall and a mixture of Tom, my dad, and Uncle David, I thought, but they both kept saying how much I was like him. I hugged Mouse till she complained, and got her fur in my eyes so they ran, and she said, *Be off now, I will miss you—but I can't say I'm unhappy, what with David being special like you and Tom, and the biggest swimming in the world right outside the door.*

It was a huge drive, back to the north, and as we journeyed, I started to feel happy and sad at the same time; sad to be leaving Uncle David's and the sea and Mouse and my new brother Tom, but happy to be going home and seeing my first brother Tom, and Mum and Gran and my friends.

Uncle David booked into the only inn, as Mum didn't have enough bedrooms—though she tried to insist on giving him hers while she would sleep "ever so cozy" in the living room—and he went and visited Tom in the hospital, who looked terrible, but apparently had taken a major turn for the better, right on the day Mum had told him that me and Mouse had arrived at Uncle David's safely, and that Mouse was to stay there as long as we needed.

I went too, and Tom clutched my hand and made me tell him the whole story, though the nurses kept saying I wasn't to tire him. Uncle David prowled around, talked to

163

doctors, and leaned over notes, sighing and rubbing his hair.

He only stayed for two nights, but he and Mum and Gran sat up talking late each time, till he walked off to the inn in the dark.

I had to go to the police station and tell my whole story so they could make a proper report. I might have forgotten to mention the bit about the ponies.

The local newspaper had splashed my "missing" story over its front page, especially as usually nothing much happened here and they had to make do with headlines like BRANCH FALLS ON ROAD IN HIGH WIND or SCOUTS CLEAR FOOTPATH. As they had helped with spreading the news of my disappearance, it was only polite I give them an exclusive interview.

They got everything wrong, of course, because they didn't listen properly, I suppose, or maybe, like Uncle David said, because they always make the story they want to tell. Anyway, the papers around the country got hold of it then, and told it even wilder, so that's why you might have read about me and Mouse, and how we rescued a toddler from drowning in a swollen river, fought with savage guard dogs, stopped half-starved wild ponies from going to slaughter, saved a whole Gypsy family—including

164

lots of babies—from a mob who were setting fire to their camper, and finally scaled a dangerous cliff to reach my uncle's house and safety.

Barney was much better after months with the dog shrink, and went to live with Uncle David, who was the only person the shrink felt he could trust to own such a dog. Mouse groaned at first when she heard he was to join her, but in no time at all, she was getting him to swim and one day, Uncle David even posted us a photograph of the two of them curled up asleep together in a dog basket.

When Tom came home from the hospital in the winter, Mum sat down with both of us at the old kitchen table and, with the smell of baking bread around us, and steam at the windows, we went through old photographs of Dad and she told us stories about him we didn't know, or had forgotten, and me and Tom tried to remember all the things he'd said and done and mostly how he'd made us laugh.

Mum phoned Uncle David once a week, or he phoned her, and when Tom was really fighting back, the next summer, nearly a whole year later, he and I went on the train to Tawntown, because we could be trusted now, and Uncle David waited on the platform for us and drove us all the rest of the way. We stayed for two whole weeks, and from then on, that was the pattern. When Tom was well, we visited Tom-my-new-brother, who now lived in a house, but still had Charlie and the ponies on a scrap of river meadow nearby. We learned to spring onto them from the ground, and gallop and reach down low to pick up sticks from a bucket in fantastic races, which sometimes we even won.

We went at Christmas, one time, too, and Daisy was back from Peru, and Dan was there and we watched slides of her travels and Dan kept making terrible jokes until we were all crying with laughter.

And, of course, when Tom had won his fight, and was really and truly, officially fine, we brought Mouse home again.

Me and Tom, of course, knew that that day was what Tom had waited for, the reason he'd hung on, the reason he'd got better. But as I said at the beginning, there's no telling some people. Like the thing about talking to dogs. Uncle David says, the main thing is never to deny who or what you are, but just don't mention it in the wrong company. Just bide your time and you will find "like kind" and then you can be truly yourself. I asked him what "like kind" meant, and he said, just people who are like you, or who understand. That was why, when I'd turned up at his door with Mouse, he didn't have to hide the fact he could talk to her and understand her. He knew I could too.

Mouse has listened to all this, now I've written it down. She's lying curled at my feet, trying to make a good headrest out of my ankle. She says:

The trouble isn't about Truth and Lies. It's about people talking a great deal more than necessary about things of no importance, and not nearly enough about the important things. Like when dinner will be ready, for the dog who has saved twelve chickens from the fox, and found a lost lamb, all in one day.

About the Author

L. S. Matthews has written poetry and short stories since she was a child. Today she writes full-time in England, where she lives with her husband and their two children. Her first book for young readers, *Fish*, was named a *Publishers Weekly* Best Book of the Year and a *Publishers Weekly* Flying Start and was a Borders Original Voices book.